国家出版基金项目
NATIONAL PUBLICATION FOUNDATION

Planned by Zhuang Zhixiang   Edited by Pan Wenguo

READINGS OF CHINESE CULTURE SERIES

— ACADEMICS III —

History as a Mirror for Governance and Chinese Historiography

Translated by Zhang Chunbai

中国经典文化走向世界丛书

学术卷 三

庄智象◎总策划   潘文国◎总主编

张春柏◎译

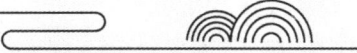

上海外语教育出版社
外教社 SHANGHAI FOREIGN LANGUAGE EDUCATION PRESS
www.sflep.com

图书在版编目(CIP)数据

中国经典文化走向世界丛书. 学术卷. 三/张春柏译.
—上海：上海外语教育出版社，2018
ISBN 978-7-5446-5536-1

I.①中… II.①张… III.①中国文学—综合作品集—英文
IV.①I211

中国版本图书馆CIP数据核字(2018)第183483号

出版发行：**上海外语教育出版社**
　　　　　　（上海外国语大学内）　邮编：200083
电　　话：021-65425300（总机）
电子邮箱：bookinfo@sflep.com.cn
网　　址：http://www.sflep.com
责任编辑：李振荣

印　　刷：**上海盛通时代印刷有限公司**
开　　本：635×965　1/16　印张 9.5　字数 152千字
版　　次：2018年11月第1版　2018年11月第1次印刷
印　　数：1 100 册

书　　号：ISBN 978-7-5446-5536-1 / B
定　　价：30.00 元

本版图书如有印装质量问题，可向本社调换
质量服务热线：4008-213-263　电子邮箱：editorial@sflep.com

"Cherish one's own beauty, respect other's beauty, and when both beauties are respected and cherished, the world will become one", said Fei Xiaotong, a famous Chinese sociologist at a celebration party in honor of his eightieth birthday about thirty years ago. In a time of growing interest in intercultural communication today, these words sound especially wise and far-sighted. Translation, as one of the most important means for cultural communication, is usually done into one's mother tongue from other languages by native translators. This largely guarantees the quality of translated text, so far as the linguistic readability is concerned. However, this method implies a one-sidedness in correspondence, as only the translator's "respect for other's beauty" is concerned, regardless, though not completely, of how the local people look upon and cherish their own beauty. It should be compensated by translations on the other way, that is, works selected, interpreted, and translated by the local people themselves into languages other than their own. This approach may go directly against the prevalent views in modern translation theories but, in my opinion, is worthy of practicing. It is perhaps an even more effective way to bring about successful communication in cultures, and the beauties of the world can really be shared by the world's people. It is with such understanding that the Shanghai Foreign Languages Education Press is organizing a new series of books, entitled *Readings of Chinese Culture*, to introduce Chinese culture, past and present, to the world, with works selected and translated by the Chinese scholars and translators.

The series will cover a wide range of writings including but not restricted to works of different literary genres. For the first batch, we are glad to provide three books of essays and one book of short stories, all written by authors of the 20th century. They will be continued by a batch of serious academic writings on premodern Chinese classics in philosophy, literature, and historiography, written by influential scholars of our time.

Later, we will offer more books on classical Chinese drama, classical Chinese poetry, etc.

Some of the books in the series have been published before, but they have been revised and rearranged for the new purpose to meet the current needs of broader readers. We are looking forward to hearing comments and suggestions on the series for future improvement.

Pan Wenguo

CONTENTS

INTRODUCTION

Through years of efforts of the authors and translators, the Chinese-English Series of Pre-modern Chinese Classics and Traditional Culture has finally come under publication. The word *pre-modern* here refers to a specific period in Chinese history between *ancient* and *modern*, starting, as I propose, from the Song Dynasty.

The Song Dynasty is a very important period in China which, in a sense, marks the end of the classical China and the beginning of the pre-modern China. Before the Song Dynasty, China had always been a society of aristocrats when all important persons known to us, even the humblest ones like Tao Yuanming or Du Fu, had an aristocratic or noble background, whereas from the Song Dynasty on, common people from grassroots might have a chance to enter the elitist gentry; in fact, certain people from poor families had even become prime ministers or esteemed scholars in the Song Dynasty. The reason is that the imperial examination system which was founded in the Sui and Tang Dynasties was brought into full play in the Song Dynasty and yielded its best effect. "A muddy-footed farmer in the morning, an official in the emperor's court in the evening" became a realizable dream and the social strata became a convective and lively one. At the same time, thanks to the imperial policy which lay more emphasis on culture than on army, education and cultural undertakings were highly encouraged, which made the Song Dynasty the most wealthy and prosperous period in the history of China or even the world. What was described in the famous genre painting of *A Clear Bright Day on the River* by Zhang Zeduan and the famous tune-poem *Watching the Sea Tide* by Liu Yong, or recorded in the memoirs of *The Prosperous Days in Kaifeng* by Meng Yuanlao and *The Past Memories of Hangzhou* by Zhou Mi reflected the thriving and vigorous civil life never found in earlier dynasties, and gave us a direct impression that the Song and the Tang belong to two different epochs with the Song much closer to us. The much talked-about "four great inventions of China", with the exception of *paper*, were achieved in the Song Dynasty and introduced to the West, leading to the great Renaissance in Europe.

Culturally speaking, the Song Dynasty is an epoch of historic importance which creates the future by inheriting the past. This is a time when all the past cultural achievements were inherited and summarized; it is also a time when people made cultural achievements to influence the coming times till today in China as well as in East Asia. It might not be everybody's knowledge that the "traditional China" or "Chinese tradition" we talk about proudly today was not that of the Han, Tang or pre-Qin as we imagine or believe, but was actually created from the Song Dynasty, or reshaped by the Song people in the name of earlier periods. For instance, in the May Fourth Movement in 1919, people raised the banner of "Down with the Kong stash (Confucian doctrines)", but their criticism should actually be targeted at the "Zhu stash", as what they repudiated was not the doctrines of Kong Zi or Meng Zi, but the doctrine of Cheng Yi and Zhu Xi, only disguised as the former. And the Confucianism or neo-Confucianism many people have been advocating since the 1930s till today is actually a resurgence of the Song-Ming Principlism. Using the method of "elaboration instead of creation", Zhu Xi successfully transformed Kong ideology into Zhu ideology, which later became the dominant ideology especially since the Ming Dynasty as it was adopted as the only authorized standard for imperial examinations. The methodology of Zhu Xi is a typical example of the Song scholars, which was adopted by other people in other fields as well. Everyone is familiar with the stories of "two Sima's". The former refers to Sima Qian in the Han Dynasty who created the chronological-biographical style in writing history, thus laying the foundation of the 25 orthodox histories in China, whereas the latter refers to Sima Guang in the Song Dynasty who, by continuing the tradition of *Spring-Autumn Annals* in the ancient time, revived the annalistic style in history writing, thus not only successfully inheriting the achievement of the past 17 *Histories*, but also opening a broader way for later history writing such as the event-focused style and the outline-focused style. Zheng Qiao of the Southern Song Dynasty found another new path by emphasizing the memorandum part of *Historical Records* and *History of the Han Dynasty* and spent his whole life finishing the book *Comprehensive Study of Memorandums*, a vital complement to Sima Guang's book which merely reorganized the biography part of *Histories*. The two books formed another tradition in historical studies, working side by side with the orthodox 25 *Histories* and impacting the historical study till today.

From the above examples we conclude that one cannot really understand China and Chinese tradition without studying the Song Dynasty and its cultural contribution. However, for a very long time in our translation and introduction of Chinese culture to the world, we lay too much emphasis on the pre-Qin part and neglect the Song Dynasty. The pre-Qin classics and philosophical works have had more than scores of translations while important books since the Song Dynasty, save poetry, plays and novels, have drawn little attention and translation. We translated *Confucian Analects* and *Mencius*, but did not know that the "feudal ideology" which had restrained the Chinese nation for centuries did not come directly from them but from the Song-Ming Principlism; we translated *Laoze* and *Zhuangzi* but did not know that what influenced the thoughts of intellectuals after the Song Dynasty was already an amalgam that merged Daoism, Confucianism and Buddhism, with the Chan Buddhism playing a very important role. Realizing this, we planned to do something to fill in the blank so as to draw attention from home and abroad to the introduction of the *pre-modern* cultural literature, of which the present series is the initial step.

The role of the Song Dynasty as a linkage between the ancient and the modern can be seen principally in the several "great" books or anthologies. In the early Northern Song period there already appeared the "four great works" of *Taiping Imperial Encyclopedia*, *Referential Records from Imperial Archives*, *Taiping Miscellany* and *Choice Blossoms of Literature*, three out of the four containing 1,000 volumes. These were doubtlessly the representative establishments of the Song culture. The *Kaibao Tripitaka* laid the foundation for the Buddhist pitaka compilation. The *Enlarged Rhyming Dictionary*, the

Collected Rhyming Dictionary, the *Enlarged Sinographic Dictionary* and the *Classified Sinographic Dictionary* marked new achievements in dictionary compilation. The *History as a Mirror for Governance* opened up a new path for historiography. The *Comprehensive Study of Memorandums* served as an important continuation in the formation of the ten *Comprehensives.* Hong Mai's *Miscellaneous Notes from the Tolerance Study,* Shen Kuo's *Pen Talk in the Dreamed Creek Garden* and Wang Yinglin's *Record of Observances from Arduous Studies* marked the beginning of pre-modern academic research. Although the *Complete Works of Zhu Xi* was compiled just recently, most of the works contained therein were already popular in the late Song Dynasty. Among them, the *Collected Annotations to the Four Books,* the *Close Reflections,* and the *Classified Analects of Zhu Xi* even became the most important textbooks of Principlism during the 700 years from the late Song Dynasty to the beginning of the 20th century. And from Zhu Xi one would naturally relate to Wang Yangming whose Mindology had played no less important role since the mid-Ming Dynasty. Thus we decided to introduce the pre-modern classics and their influence to Chinese culture by way of introducing some "great books" and their developments. In the present series we have chosen six books. They are respectively, the *Complete Works of Zhu Xi,* the *Records of Instructions and Reviews,* the *History as a Mirror for Governance,* the *Choice Blossoms of Literature,* the *Taiping Miscellany,* and the *Buddhist Tripitaka.* And we invited established experts in relevant areas to write concise, introductory books in the manner of "big heads preparing small pamphlets", before asking English experts with Chinese study background to translate them into English. Specifically, the authors and translators of the six books are:

> *Complete Works of Zhu Xi and Its Inheritance,* written by Fu Huisheng, annotated & translated by Pan Wenguo
>
> *To Attain Innate Knowledge — Records of the Instructions and Reviews and Yangming's Mindology,* written by Yang Guorong, translated by Gong Haiyan
>
> *History as a Mirror for Governance and Chinese Historiography,*

written by Zhuang Huiming, translated by Zhang Chunbai

Choice Blossoms of Literature and the Trends of Pre-modern Poetry and Prose, written by Chen Yinchi, translated by Zhang Deshao

The Buddhist Triptaka in Chinese and Its Cultural Concern, written by Li Xiangping, translated by Fu Huisheng

You may find in the list not a few names very familiar to the academic circles. For example, Professor Yang Guorong is the Changjiang Scholar of the State Ministry of Education and dean of the School of Humanities and Social Sciences of East China Normal University (ECNU), Professor Zhuang Huiming is the ex-vice-president of ECNU and dean of Meng Xiancheng Academy, Professor Chen Yinchi is head of the Department of Chinese Language and Literature of Fudan University and "Talent of the New Century" assigned by the State Ministry of Education, Professor Chen Dakang is the former head of the Department of Chinese Language and Literature, former head of the ECNU Library as well as member of the Discipline Appraisal Group of the Degree Committee of the State Council, Professor Li Xiangping is head of the Department of Sociology of ECNU and vice-chairman of Shanghai Society for Religious Studies, Professor Zhang Chunbai is the former dean of the School of Foreign Languages of ECNU and member of the Guidance Committee for Teaching Foreign Languages of the State Ministry of Education, as well as the vice chairman of the Shanghai Society of Foreign Languages, Professor Fu Huisheng is head of the Department of International Chinese Studies of ECNU and standing council member of China Association for Comparative Studies between English and Chinese, so on and so forth. Their participation is an important guarantee of the success of the present series. Here I would like to express my personal gratitude to these eminent scholars!

The plan for this series actually started a dozen of years ago and many authors handed their manuscripts rather early. It's mainly my delay and the difficulty in translation that had kept the process so long. Now, with the efforts of all the authors and translators, this series is finally under publication. Special thanks must go to Professor Fu Huisheng who personally took up the writing of one book and the translation of another two books. Besides, he has helped me to read over most of the manuscripts of translations. Without his persistence the series would not be successful.

Finally, I would like to extend my thanks to Shanghai Foreign Language Education Press and its president and editor-in-chief, Professor Zhuang Zhixiang, who has been unswervingly in support of the country's foreign languages teaching cause, and who, in recent years, has shown special concern for promoting the traditional Chinese culture to the world. Without their support, this seemingly unpopular title would not have an opportunity to go to the public.

Pan Wenguo
Shanghai
June 28, 2016

Chapter One

The Origin and Evolution of the Annals

Nine centuries ago, in the first year of the Shaosheng Period of Emperor Zhezong (1094) of the Northern Song Dynasty, there was a heated debate between two groups of high officials over a book that had just been carved for printing. One party, headed by Prime Minister Cai Bian, insisted on destroying the printing blocks, while the other, represented by Chen Guan, the Erudite of the Imperial Ceremonials, argued that the very idea of destroying them would be a blasphemy against the late emperor Shenzong (1068–1085), who had personally written the preface to the book. Thanks to Chen Guan's argument, this book was preserved and has been handed down.

The narrowly surviving book is *History as a Mirror for Governance*[1], the first comprehensive annalistic historical record of ancient China, at which the famous historian Sima Guang[2] and his assistants had worked for nineteen years.

This magnum opus has received extremely high accolades since its publication. Emperor Shenzong, for example, gave his generous commendation: "This book is simply without parallel, by far superior to even Xun Yue's[3] *Annals of the Han Dynasty*."

---

[1] *History as a Mirror for Governance*, or *Zizhi Tongjian*, is a groundbreaking work in Chinese historiography. It records Chinese history from 403 BC to 959 AD, covering 16 dynasties and spanning across almost 1,400 years, and contains 3 million Chinese characters in 294 volumes. Sima Guang (1019 – 1086) led the compilation of the work at the order of Emperor Yingzong of the Song Dynasty.

[2] Sima Guang (1019 – 1086), courtesy name Junshi, a historian, writer and scholar-official. He was the lead compiler of the monumental history work *History as a Mirror for Governance*.

[3] Xun Yue (148 – 209), courtesy name Zhongyu, an official, historian and Confucian scholar of the Eastern Han Dynasty.

Hu Sansheng, a renowned scholar of the early Yuan Dynasty, commented, "Without any knowledge of this book, an emperor would not know how to govern his people and prevent instability, an official would not know how to serve the emperor and help him govern the people, and the common people would not be able to do anything without bringing disgrace to their ancestors, nor could they ever expect to leave a name in history."

Wang Mingsheng of the Qing Dynasty was even more lavish with his praise, "This is a book of necessity for the world, and a must for any scholar."

Cen Zhongmian said a few decades ago, "*History as a Mirror for Governance* is an outstanding general history of China that is second to none in the method of compilation, the richness of contents, the exhaustiveness of textual study, the succinctness of language, and the comprehensiveness of comments."

Despite the different perspectives of the people in different historical periods, the unfailing attention and praises this book has enjoyed in the past nine centuries point clearly to its extraordinary status in Chinese culture and its tremendous political, cultural, and psychological influence on the later ages.

What kind of history book, then, is *History as a Mirror for Governance*? And what influence has this annalistic history exerted on the development of Chinese historiography and the thought of Chinese people? To answer these questions, one has to trace the origin and development of the annalistic style of historiography before the Song Dynasty.

Human society has existed from time immemorial. In a broad sense, it is as long as the history of man himself. There were, however, no historical records of the events and activities of people until written language came into being. The oldest of such historical documents were annals.

1. The Origin of the Annals

Annals are records of historical events written in chronological order. World historiography, including that of China, shows that the chronological way of recording was the earliest method man used to record history, hence the origin of all ancient history books.

In Greece, *The Histories*, or *Histories of Greco-Persian Wars* written by Herodotus, who is acclaimed as "father of history", in 430 B.C., was in the annalistic style. *History of the Peloponnesian War* by Thucydides in 441 B.C. was also written in this style. In Germany, the earliest history books included *Annals* by Lambert von Hersfeld and *Annals of the World* by Ekkehart von Aura. In England, both *An Ecclesiastical History of the English People* written by Saint Bede, the "father of English history", and *The Anglo-Saxon Chronicle* were written in this way, too. In Russia, the earliest history book was *The Primary Chronicle* by Saint Nestor. All these books show that the earliest history books published in the West were generally in the annalistic style.

In China, the annalistic style of historiography dates back to the Shang (17th century B.C. – 11th century B.C.) and Zhou (11th century B.C. – 256B.C.) Dynasties. The earliest existing written records in China are the inscriptions on bones or tortoise shells, which are the most primitive official archives inscribed for certain events. From the point of view of historiography, they are not strictly historical records, but they can be considered the embryos of annals since many of them were recorded chronologically.

China had a strict system of official historians in ancient times. Many descriptions of such a system can be found in the historical records of the Shang and Zhou Dynasties, which have been proven reliable. There were two categories of official historians: One in charge of recording divinations, astronomical phenomena and calendars, and the other in charge of drafting royal orders, recording the words and deeds of emperors and princes, and keeping documents and archives. According to the *Bibliography* in *the Book of the Han Dynasty* by Ban Gu, there were two types of official historians, i.e. "left historiographers" whose duty it was to record what emperors and high officials said in the court, and "right historiographers" who were responsible for documenting important events. While the existence of this strict division of duties remains a question, it is clear that, official historians in ancient China did have the responsibility of recording the words and deeds of emperors and princes. Those officials developed a common practice of documenting certain events. According to the renowned scholar Wang Guowei, "In the Shang and Zhou Dynasties, historical events were recorded in the order of date, month and year." (*Collected Writings by Guantang*, vol.1)

After the Zhou Dynasty replaced the Shang Dynasty, the central government appointed a grand historian in charge of historical records and contemporary official documents, and sent some other official historians to various vassal states to verify their official documents as governmental archives. In the *Rituals* made by the Duke of Zhou (1100 B.C.-?), some basic principles were established for the recording of events. One of them was to record events in the order of date, month, season and year.

This format for the official documentation of the royal orders and the treaties between vassal states contained all the rudiments of annals, though it was not meant for the writing of history books. If the chronological records by the ancient official historians were the embryos of annals in ancient China, the birth of the annalistic style of historiography was marked by Kong zi' *Spring and Autumn Annals*.

Kong zi' family was originally a noble family in the State of Song. As it lost power in political struggles, the family had to go into exile in the State of Lu and eventually settled down in Zouyi, which is part of today's city of Qufu. Kong zi himself was once a petty official in charge of granaries, oxen and sheep. For some time he was mayor of the capital and Minister of Justice of the State of Lu. Later, he left the State and visited other principalities in an effort to disseminate his political ideals, but none of the princes and vassals accepted them. Kong zi then devoted his energies to education and the editing work of ancient books and records. He made an indelible contribution to the writing, preservation and dissemination of some of the major ancient books and records. One of them is the *Spring and Autumn Annals*[1], which is the first history book written in the annalistic

---

[1] *The Spring and Autumn Annals*, or *Chun Qiu*, is an ancient Chinese chronicle that covers a 241-year period from 722 to 481 BC. It is the earliest surviving Chinese historical text to be arranged in the form of annals. Because it was traditionally regarded as having been compiled by Kong Zi (Confucius), it was included as one of the Confucian Five Classics.

style in the world.

The use of the words "*Spring and Autumn*" in the title of the book was a tradition of official historians rather than a creation by Kong zi himself. In fact, during the Spring and Autumn Period (770–476 B.C.), many principalities had their own histories, most of which contained these words in their titles. Mo Di, the founder of Mohism, claimed that he had read the "*Spring-and-Autumns*" of nearly all the states, including those of the States of Zhou, Yan, Song and Qi. Meng Zi also pointed out that *sheng* (meaning "history") of the State of Jin, *zhi* (meaning "records") of the State of Zheng, *taowu* (meaning "legends") of the State of Chu, and "*spring and autumn*" of the State of Lu were the same in nature, despite their different names.

Kong zi' *Spring and Autumn Annals* was based on an older version of the history of Lu, but he assimilated some of the elements from the histories of the other states as well. Once he visited the Royal Library of the Zhou Dynasty and read some relevant documents there. Meanwhile, he sent over a dozen disciples, including Zixia, to other states, who brought back the history of the Zhou Dynasty as well as "the precious records of a hundred and more principalities" for reference. Thus, the *Spring and Autumn Annals* is not just the history of one single state, but a full record of the whole historical period of 242 years from 722 to 481 B.C., covering the major historical events of other states as well as those of Lu, though it was chiefly based on the latter and on the reign titles of the dukes of Lu for the recording of events.

A much "simplified" version of the older history of Lu, the *Spring and Autumn Annals* is marked by laconic brevity. The average length of the entries is a little over a dozen words, the longest one being forty-five words, some having only dates. The whole book records the history of 242 years with only a little more than 18,000 words. This excessively laconic way of recording gave rise to many criticisms later. Huan Tan of the Eastern Han Dynasty (25–220A.D.), for instance, said that it resisted the understanding of even those sages who had spent ten years pondering over it. Wang Anshi, a prime minister of the Song Dynasty dismissed it as "a hotchpotch of recorded events". Ji Yun, a scholar of the Qing Dynasty, also said that no one, not even sages, could see the reasons for the praises and criticisms of certain events in the book without knowing the events themselves.

Nevertheless, despite all the praises and criticisms since the Warring States Period (475–221 B.C.), there is no denying that the book enjoys an important position in the development of historiography in ancient China.

As the first history book of the annalistic style, Kong zi' *Spring and Autumn Annals* made many indelible contributions to the historiography of later dynasties, two of which deserve our special attention. One is the fact that it successfully converted the original documentation of ancient historians into historical records by combining *"purpose"*, *"events"* and *"words"* coherently. *"Purpose"* here refers to the purpose and views in editing history books; *"events"* refers to historical facts to be recorded; and *"words"* refers to the language used to record the writers' views and historical events. The Spring and Autumn Period and the Warring States Period witnessed the first upsurge of cultural development in China. From the very start, various schools of thought that emerged during this period showed great scholarly concerns for social politics and thus formed a cultural tradition, that is, the unfailing attachment of great importance to social politics in academic studies. As the founder of Confucianism, Kong zi himself had clear political purposes in mind when he was writing the *Spring and Autumn Annals*. Meng Zi said that treacherous ministers would be awed on hearing this book. Dong Zhongshu, a prime minister of the Western Han Dynasty (221 B.C.-25 A.D.), even remarked that the book was the ultimate source of social order and justice and the best resource available to restore order and justice in a disordered society. It can thus be seen that the ultimate aim of the book was the restoration of the kingly way and the rectification of names. To achieve this purpose, Kong zi ignored the old tradition of "recording whatever the monarchs and princes did", and selected and arranged those historical events which met his purpose. Consequently, minor events that had some bearing on this purpose were recorded, whereas some major events that had no relevance with it were omitted. In this book, Kong zi expressed his praises and criticisms about the historical events. He severely criticized the improper behavior of the sons of heaven (emperors), denounced those princes and vassals who had overstepped their authorities, and condemned the ministers who had usurped or attempted to usurp the throne. His purpose was to exhort people to be good and guard them against evils in order to establish the kingly way through the presentation of historical events. Thus, his *Spring and Autumn Annals* created a precedent for Chinese historical study in attaching importance to social politics and serving political needs.

The other important contribution of Kong zi' book was the establishment of the general principles of the annalistic style in historiography. The whole book was written in clear chronological order. All the events that took place in the 242 years, including the official visits and invitations, the alliances, and the wars between various principalities, as well as natural events such as solar eclipses, earthquakes, landfalls, floods and droughts, were recorded in the order of year, month, and date. If the date was unclear, the names of year, season and month would be recorded; and in case the month was unclear, there were year and season. It was influenced by the official historians in the method of recording the events, but Kong zi made some inventions. Wang Guowei, for instance, found in his textual research that between the Shang and Zhou Dynasties, time was written in the order of date, month and year, and that official historians of the Shang Dynasty sometimes omitted the names of the years. In the inscriptions on bronze objects that were made in the early Zhou Dynasty, months appeared before dates, but years still came last. Kong zi made it a rule to record events in the strict order of year, month and date. Compared with the inscriptions on bones, tortoise shells, and bronze objects which were either too miscellaneous or recorded only a few isolated events, and with *the History of Qin* in which the events had no dates or months, *Spring and Autumn Annals* was much more systematic in the recording of historical events with authorial comments. This is one of the most important hallmarks of the annalistic historical documents.

Besides, Kong zi changed the recording of time in previous historical documents and used the order of year, month and date for the sake of clarity in his own narration. Sima Qian said in the Preface to the Hereditary Table of the Three Dynasties in the *Records of the Historian*, "Kong zi edited the *Spring and Autumn Annals* based on historical documentation, and corrected the order of year, season, month and date in old documents." This shows that the establishment of this order is not only an important part of Kong zi' work but also one of his major contributions to Chinese historiography. It was proved later that the determination of the chronological order of the historical events was the most difficult and, indeed, the most important part of the work without which there would be no annalistic histories. The establishment of the order of year, month and date in the *Spring and Autumn Annals* marked the birth of the annalistic style of historiography.

2. The Improvement of the Annals during the Warring States Period

If the birth of the annalistic style of historiography is marked by the *Spring and Autumn Annals*, its development should be attributed to *Zuo Zhuan*, which is also translated as *Zuo's Commentary*[1]. Originally named *Zuo's Spring and Autumn Annals*, the book *Zuo's Commentary* assumed its present name in the Eastern Han Dynasty. Its authorship still remains unclear. Generally it is acknowledged to have been written by Zuo Qiuming, a grand historian of the State of Lu towards the end of the Spring and Autumn Period. Some scholars suggested that it might have been written by a certain descendent of Yi Xiang, a left historiographer of Chu, or by the famous military strategist Wu Qi. Still another guess is that it was possibly written by Liu Xin of the Han Dynasty. The famous scholar Gu Yanwu[2] of the early Qing Dynasty held the view that it was not written by any

---

① *Zuo's Commentary*, or *Zuo Zhuan*, is an ancient Chinese narrative history traditionally regarded as a commentary on *The Spring and Autumn Annals*. It covers a period from 722 to 468 BC, and focuses on the political, diplomatic, and military affairs of that era.
② Gu Yanwu (1613 – 1682), also called Master Tinglin, a philologist and geographer in the late Ming Dynasty to the early Qing Dynasty. He has a famous saying, "Everybody is responsible for the fate of the world."

one single person in one single generation. According to him, it was the fruit of the continuous efforts of a number of scholars throughout many generations. This opinion sounds more convincing. As a matter of fact, it is commonly acknowledged in academic circles that many important books and records that appeared in the Spring and Autumn Period were written by more than one person in more than one generation's time. The same was probably true of *Zuo's Commentary*. Most scholars in this field of learning hold that it was probably compiled by a number of people in the early years of the Warring States Period on the basis of the historical records of those vassal states. Its obscure authorship, however, does not affect people's study and evaluation of this book.

Like the *Spring and Autumn Annals*, *Zuo's Commentary* is also a historical record in the annalistic style, but it is more extensive and exhaustive. Like the *Spring and Autumn Annals*, *Zuo's Commentary* dated historical events in accordance with the reign titles of the twelve princes of the State of Lu, from the first year of the reign of Duke Yin (722 B.C.) to the twenty-seventh year of the reign of Duke Ai (468 B.C.), which was fourteen years longer than that in the *Spring and Autumn Annals*. Some of the events mentioned or described in the book took place as early as in the twenty-third year of the reign of King Xuan of the Zhou Dynasty (805 B.C.) or as late as in the fourteenth year of the reign of Duke Dao of Lu (454 B.C.). The whole book covers a span of time that is over one century longer than *the Spring and Autumn Annals* does. Moreover, it contains over 180,000 words while the *Spring and Autumn Annals* has only 18,000 words, which reflects the difference in the degree of detailedness between the two books.

The relationship between *Zuo's Commentary* and the *Spring and Autumn Annals* is so close that many scholars have suggested over the centuries that the former was written as a sort of interpretation of the latter. It is one between a classic and its commentary, just like the inside and outside of a coat which are mutually complementary and inseparable from each other, though linguistically the former is short and pithy, whereas the latter is lengthy and extensive.

There is yet another opinion that *Zuo's Commentary* is an independent history work. After Confucianism gained the dominant position in the political and academic lives of the country in the reign of Emperor Wudi of the Han Dynasty, the *Spring and Autumn Annals* was exalted as a classic while *Zuo's Commentary* was considered one of its three best existing commentaries, the other two being *Gongyang's Commentary* and *Guliang's Commentary*. It has been pointed out that there is a considerable number of disagreements and discrepancies between the two books, as each has some contents that are absent in the other, and while Kong zi' book records mainly the history of the State of Lu, *Zuo's Commentary* records many events that took place in the State of Jin; moreover, there are more obvious disagreements in political views. Therefore, *Zuo's Commentary* could not be a commentary on the *Spring and Autumn Annals*.

As each side has its reasons, it is difficult to reach the final conclusion. It is beyond doubt, however, that the two books are closely related to and yet somewhat different from each other. It should also be fully recognized that *Zuo's Commentary* is more mature, more exhaustive and richer in historical materials than the *Spring and Autumn Annals*.

Like the *Spring and Autumn Annals*, *Zuo's Commentary* dates events in the order of year, season, month, and day, but there is much improvement in the way the events are recorded. While the former records only the outlines of the events without any details, like a journal account of major events, the latter not only records the courses of the events, but also describes the characters' looks, deeds, and thoughts, and discusses their causes and consequences as thoroughly as possible, which reveals the social reality of the time. For instance, the former records the famous Chengpu Battle (632 B.C.) between the States of Jin and Chu in only a little more than one hundred words, whereas the latter uses several thousand words recording the causes and course of the battle and describing the images of Duke Wen of Jin and the Chu general Ziyu, which greatly enhances the value of the historical record.

The Spring and Autumn Period was a time of violent social disturbances caused by unprecedentedly complicated social contradictions. With the decline of the Zhou Dynasty, there were incessant wars between those big principalities for hegemony and amalgamation. In order to reveal the inherent laws of history, *Zuo's Commentary* devotes much effort to the recording of the wars, with descriptions of almost every aspect of the individual battles, from the preparations to the making of strategic decisions, to the fierce fighting on the battlefields and the results. The descriptions are coherent and well-arranged, written in simple but graceful language, which greatly enhances the readability and credibility of the historical accounts, in sharp contrast with the monotonous style of the *Spring and Autumn Annals*. All this marks the maturity of the annalistic style of historiography.

It should also be mentioned that *Zuo's Commentary* is characterized by the integration of narrative discourse with authorial comments. Kong zi' *Spring and Autumn Annals* is distinguished by its "pithy language with extensive allusions". It often expresses the author's views on the nature of the events and the people involved in extremely simple language. This style of Kong zi' was later known as "Spring and Autumn style", that is, the technique of intimating moral judgments in the smallest possible number of words. This method, however, has an apparent drawback: It not only restricts the expression of the author's ideas and makes it difficult to give detailed accounts of historical events, but also tends to make the comments obscure and even undecipherable. *Zuo's Commentary*, as an improvement, adopts the method of combining the narration of historical events with authorial comments.

One can easily find in *Zuo's Commentary* that the author makes direct and indirect comments on historical events in three different ways. The first is through direct comments introduced by the clause "The superior man remarks". There are altogether over fifty such direct comments in the book, most of which directly express the author's attitude towards the events regarding etiquette and propriety. For example, after a description of how the royal family of the Zhou Dynasty exchanged hostages with the State of Zheng, the "superior man's remark" goes: The exchange of hostages would be meaningless if mutual trust is not gained through honest deeds. It goes further that if the two parties exercised self-restraint with etiquette and sense of propriety and righteousness, and put themselves in each other's shoes, then no one could possibly set them against each other even without the hostages, and that a "superior man" could unite two states by practicing etiquette instead of exchanging hostages. It was due to the distrust between the King of the Zhou Dynasty and the princes that he exchanged hostages with Duke Zhuang of the State of Zheng in the third year of the reign of the Duke Yin of the State of Lu (720 B.C.). However, what happened later proved that it did not have any restraint on the behavior of either party. This comment, being a direct criticism of both the King and Duke Zheng, is an unequivocal statement of the author's political attitude.

The second type of comments is made by quoting or forging the sayings of wise people of previous times. Such comments on historical events are pervasive in *Zuo's Commentary*. According to the record, for example, Zichan, a renowned politician of the State of Zheng, said on his deathbed in the twentieth year of the reign of Duke Zhao of Lu (522 B.C.), "Only virtuous rulers can govern his people with lenient policies as their first choice, and stern policies as their second choice." This means that one must combine these two kinds of policies in the governance of a country. The author is obviously highly appreciative of this, but instead of making direct comments, he quotes Kong zi, "Well said! Overly lenient policies breed unruliness in the people, which should be corrected with stern measures; on the other hand, overly stern policies will hurt people, who should therefore be placated with lenient policies. In other words, in governing the people, one should use stern policies to supplement lenient policies, which in turn should be combined with stern policies." Here, the author is apparently expressing his own attitude through Kong zi' mouth. The author also believes that Kong zi said after Zichan's death, "His kindheartedness is reminiscent of ancient sages." Some scholars suspect that it is a pure forgery. However, no matter whether Kong zi actually said it or not, the author's intention is clear, that is, to express his own opinions with the help of Kong zi' prestige.

The third way of making comments on historical events in *Zuo's*

Commentary is quoting the words of the people involved or other influential people instead of making direct authorial comments. Such examples are also abundant in the book. A typical example is the dialogue between Shusun Bao, Senior Minister of the State of Lu, and Fan Xuanzi, Senior Minister of the State of Jin, when the former was on an official visit to Jin in the twenty-fourth year of the reign of Duke Xiang of Lu (549 B.C.). Shusun Bao is quoted as saying, "I heard that Zang Wenzhong, the late senior official of Lu, had said that the supreme thing was the setting up of standards of virtuous conduct; the next best thing was noble service to the country; and the third best was achieving glory by writing. Only these three accomplishments can be considered immortal, whereas the preservation of the family line and the honors being handed down from generation to generation cannot be considered immortal." It can thus be seen that the author of *Zuo's Commentary* is in complete agreement with Shusun Bao. By quoting Shusun Bao's words, the author is advocating an outlook on life with moral virtues at its core. He expounds in extremely pithy language the moral spirit of the traditional Chinese culture which attaches great importance to moral virtues, devotion to one's country, and the writing of immortal works, which is exactly what the author advocates.

Of the three different ways of making authorial comments on historical events, the first one, i.e. the fifty-odd direct comments in the book mentioned above, has exerted the most far-reaching influence on the style of the annals of later dynasties; in other words, it made the most outstanding improvements in the writing of annals on the basis of the *Spring and Autumn Annals*. The authorial comments beginning with "The superior man remarks" express the author's opinions directly. Such a close combination of narratives and comments helps to sum up the general trend of historical development. In this respect, it is far superior to the *Spring and Autumn Annals*. The differences between the two books, needless to say, do not mean that their authors have opposite attitudes and opinions. In fact, one can clearly perceive through them the gradual deepening of the historians' understanding of history and the breakthroughs in the annalistic style of historiography established by Kong zi' *Spring and Autumn Annals*.

Besides *Zuo's Commentary*, there is a number of other annalistic history books written in the Warring States Period such as *The Bamboo Annals*[①], *Gongyang's Commentary* and *Guliang's Commentary*. *The Bamboo Annals* was discovered in the Western Jin Dynasty. Judging from its contents, it is an annalistic history of the State of Wei in the Warring States Period. The other two books, being interpretations of the *Spring and Autumn Annals*, were naturally similar to the latter in style. All these books prove from another angle that the annalistic style of historiography experienced some significant developments both in the number of books completed and the method of writing in the Warring States Period.

3. The Slow Development and Stagnation of the Annalistic Style of Historiography in the Han and Tang Dynasties

As we have seen, the annals, being the earliest kind of history books in China, appeared in the Spring and Autumn Period and experienced continual developments in the Warring States Period. In the Han and Tang Dynasties, however, they went through a tortuous process from gradual maturation to slow development and even standstill.

This change started with the *Records of the Historian*[②] by Sima Qian[③].

Universally acknowledged as an immortal historian, Sima Qian was born into a family of historians engaged in the recording of the history of the Zhou Dynasty. His father Sima Tan was a versatile scholar with a good knowledge of many other fields of learning besides history. Brought up in this family tradition, Sima Qian decided to fulfill his father's will and

---

① *The Bamboo Annals*, or *Zhushu Jinian*, is an ancient Chinese chronicle that covers a period from the legendary times of the Yellow Emperor to 229 BC. Its texts today are either incomplete or of disputed authenticity.

② *Records of the Grand Historian*, or *Shiji*, is the first Chinese history work in the *Jizhuanti*-style (which records history in a series of biographies). It was begun by Sima Tan in the late 2nd century BC and finished by his son Sima Qian in around 94 BC. It sets the model for all the subsequent dynastic histories of China.

③ Sima Qian (circa 145 BC – circa 86 BC), a historian of the early Han Dynasty. He is the author of the influential history work *Records of the Grand Historian*, or *Shiji*, which covers more than 2,000 years from the legendary Yellow Emperor to his time, during the reign of Emperor Wu of the Han Dynasty.

started to write the *Records of the Historian* after he succeeded to his father as Grand Historian. With his profound knowledge, rich experiences, and vocational convenience, he immersed himself in the writing of the book with unswerving determination, even after he was thrown into prison and suffered the humiliating punishment of castration as an implicated offender in the treason case of Li Ling. After a whole decade of sustained effort, Sima Qian finally accomplished his work, which was to be recognized as an immortal monument in the history of Chinese or even world historiography.

Unlike his predecessors, Sima Qian insisted that a book of history or historical studies should bear the stamp of the historian's personal style, or "the original language and views of the writer". Inspired by this idea, he created the chronological-biographical style in writing the *Records of the Historian.*

As was mentioned above, the historical records written in the Spring and Autumn Period and the Warring States Period were mostly annals, which dominated Chinese historiography in the whole pre-Qin period. However, despite their indelible contribution as the first kind of history books, they inevitably had some inherent flaws due to their pioneering nature. Specifically, annals had two main shortcomings. One is that they are not conducive to the presentation of the cause-and-result relations of historical events. The other is that they failed to reflect the roles and statuses of important historical figures. Such deficiencies of annals gave Sima Qian inspirations for an entirely new framework of historical records, which finally led to the creation of his unique personal style. He replaced the annalistic style represented by the *Spring and Autumn Annals* and *Zuo's Commentary* with five forms of writing, i.e. chronicles, tables, records, histories of aristocratic families, and biographies of important historical figures, as the chronological-biographical style.

The most distinctive feature of such chronological-biographical histories is the fact that they focus on various historical figures and reflect their activities through their own words and deeds. This is a great creation of Sima Qian on the basis of the methods of his predecessors.

In his famous book *Generalities on History*, Liu Zhiji of the Tang Dynasty summarized the features of chronological-biographical histories as follows: The chronicles gave overall pictures of major events, and the biographies described the people in greater detail; the tables gave a brief list of major events, while the records took care of all the rest. As chronological-biographical histories were more comprehensive and inclusive than annals in the recording of historical events, the appearance of the *Records of the Historian* naturally undermined the dominant position of annals.

Following Sima Qian, Ban Gu[1] of the Eastern Han Dynasty wrote a dynastic history in a series of biographies, i.e., the *Book of the Han Dynasty*[2] in imitation of Sima Qian's book, which further improved the chronological-biographical style of history. A comparison of the contents in the two books reveals that the *Book of the Han Dynasty* not only assimilated the merits of the *Records of the Historian* but also made some improvements in style and layout. For instance, the *Records of the Historian* does not even have a "Chronicle of Emperor Huidi", though the chronicles of emperors are an important part of the book. It merely mentioned the reign of this emperor in the "Chronicle of Empress Lü". In his book, Ban Gu made up this deficiency, and thus established "the tradition of writing the chronicles of the emperors". In the titles of biographies in the *Records of the Historian*, Sima Qian used their family names, meanings of given names, official positions and even their titles of nobility inconsistently, though they were meant to convey appreciative or depreciative implications. In the *Book of the Han Dynasty*, with the exception of the chronicles of emperors, kings and princes, all the biographies are titled with the family names or full names of the people under description. Moreover, unlike in the *Records of the Historian*, where the biographies are arranged sometimes in chronological sequence, sometimes in terms of the nature of the activities recorded, and sometimes even according to when they were written, without a logical

---

(1) Ban Gu (32 – 92), a historian and poet best known for his part in compiling *The Book of Han*. He also wrote a number of *fu* (part prose and part poetry, a dominant literary form of the Han Dynasty).

(2) *The Book of Han* is a history work covering the Western Han Dynasty (206 BC – 23 AD), so it is also called *The Book of Former Han*. It was composed by Ban Gu with the help of his sister Ban Zhao, who modeled their work on Sima Qian's *Records of the Grand Historian*.

principle, the *Book of the Han Dynasty* arranges the biographies mainly in chronological order. Other factors being equal, the chronicles of emperors come first, the biographies of aristocrats come second, followed by those of famous minority people, and the last one is the "Biography of Wang Mang"; these established the precedent of putting the chronicles of emperors and the biographies of aristocrats before those of "rebels" in orthodox histories. Furthermore, this book changed "record" into "bibliography" and, by changing the "eight records" into "ten bibliographies", set an example for histories written later.

With the publication of Ban Gu's *Book of the Han Dynasty*, the chronological-biographical history greeted a new upsurge. It gradually replaced the annals and became the mainstream history in the Han and Tang Dynasties. Many important works such as the *Book of the Sui Dynasty*, and *Bibliographies of Classics* and *Bibliographic Treatises* in the history books, and other catalogue books even placed chronological-biographical histories as orthodox histories before other history books, and relegated annals to "ancient histories" or "non-official histories". Besides, the ratio between the two kinds of history books also changed. According to the history section of *A Bibliography of Classics and Books* in the *Book of the Sui Dynasty*, 67 "orthodox histories" and chronological-biological books in 3,083 volumes were published from the two Han Dynasties to the Northern and Southern Dynasties. Besides, there were also 80 histories in 4,030 volumes that were lost. In contrast, there were only 34 "ancient history books" (i.e. annals) in 666 volumes. Thus we can see that there are only half as many annals as "orthodox histories", or one sixth as many in terms of volumes. It is now clear that in the development of historical literature in China, the period between the Han Dynasty and the Northern and Southern Dynasties witnessed the rapid development of chronological-biographical histories and their surpassing of annals, not only in their status as reflected in the archives of history books, but also in terms of number.

This, nevertheless, does not mean that no significant annals were published in this period. In fact, there *was* a number of influential annals among the 34 mentioned above. A good example is the *Annals of the Latter*

Han Dynasty by Yuan Hong of the Jin Dynasty, which is an annalistic history of the 195-year Eastern Han Dynasty. Written before the *Book of the Latter Han Dynasty*① by Fan Ye②, it contains some of the historical materials that are even more valuable than those in some of the orthodox history books. When discussing history books on the Latter Han Dynasty, Liu Zhiji③ equated the *Annals of the Latter Han Dynasty* with the *Book of the Latter Han Dynasty*, which is a clear index of its academic status. In addition, some of the dynastic annals such as the *Annals of the Han and Jin Dynasties*④ by Xi Zaochi of the Jin Dynasty and the *Annals of the Jin Dynasty* by Gan Bao also had fairly high academic value. All this shows that the annalistic style of history was still in a slow process of development although it had lost its status as the mainstream style of historiography.

The most noteworthy annals published in this period is perhaps the *Annals of the Han Dynasty* by Xun Yue of the Eastern Han Dynasty, which records the rise and fall of the 210-year-long Western Han Dynasty from its founding by Emperor Liu Bang to the usurpation of the throne by Wang Mang in thirty volumes.

Born of an eminent family in the Prefecture of Yingchuan, Xun Yue served as director of the Palace Library under the reign of Emperor Xiandi. In the third year of the Jian'an Period (198 A.D.), he received the imperial order to adapt the *Book of the Han Dynasty* to annals. Accordingly, he carefully selected the key events and typical materials and trimmed off those less important ones. The whole book uses the chronicles in the *Book of the Han Dynasty* as its key link and places all the biographies, tables, bibliographies and other relevant historical materials under relevant dates. Compared with the voluminous *Book of the Han Dynasty*, which has over 800,000 words, Xun Yue's book is only one-fourth its length, with about

---

① *The Book of the Later Han* is a history work covering the history of the Han Dynasty from 6 to 189 AD. It was compiled by Fan Ye et. al. in the 5th century.

② Fan Ye (398 – 445), courtesy name Weizong, a historian of the Southern and Northern Dynasties. He compiled the history work *The Book of the Later Han*.

③ Liu Zhiji (661 – 721), courtesy name Zixuan, a historian of the Tang Dynasty well-known for his work *Shitong*.

④ *The Annals of Han*, a history work by Xun Yue (148 – 209), covering the period of 206 BC – 9 AD in the Western Han Dynasty.

200,000 words, and yet all the important systems, personages, and events are retained. His ability in condensation and synthesization, as well as his skills in citing apt examples and using pithy language, were highly praised by later historians.

Most important of all, the *Annals of the Han Dynasty* promoted the maturity and development of the annalistic style of historiography with the author's innovations while keeping the major features of the *Spring and Autumn Annals* and *Zuo's Commentary*.

As the first annalistic history adapted from a chronological-biographical history, the *Annals of the Han Dynasty* adopted the fine compilation method of the chronological-biographical history, and thus shook off the old rules of recording historical events in strict chronological order and established a more flexible way of writing annals. While following the general chronological order, the author was able to present the lives of important historical figures and the complete stories of important events without reducing them to monotonous journal accounts of events. In recording the deeds of historical figures, he made an attempt to paint a complete picture of their lives by supplementing the chronological method with flashbacks to indicate the dates of their births and some other activities. In this way, the strong point of the chronological-biographical history in writing about people was successfully applied to the writing of annals, thus opening a new way for its development.

As regards historical events, the *Annals of the Han Dynasty* further improved the method of recording them "by classification" which had been used in the *Spring and Autumn Annals* and *Zuo's Commentary*. As Xun Yue himself put it, his method was "classifying the events and putting them together under certain dates", that is, putting similar historical events together at different levels like a chain. For example, in the second year of the Yuanguang Period (133 B.C.), Emperor Wudi called a special meeting on how to counterattack the invasion of the Huns. Instead of recording it as an isolated event, this book gives a clear account of the history of the Hun nationality, as well as the battles against them by the army of Han, with an appendix of the proposals of Zhufu Yan and others against the punitive expedition against the Huns. In this way, the events were "chained" together and classified at different levels, which greatly enhanced the completeness and coherence of the stories. This method had also been used in the *Spring and Autumn Annals* and *Zuo's Commentary*, though only occasionally. The *Annals of the Han Dynasty* uses it throughout the whole book skillfully, with appendices for the first time.

One of the shortcomings of the annalistic style of history is its inability to describe personages and record events without clear dates. This drawback remained in *Zuo's Commentary*, in which some of the events that should have been recorded had to be omitted regrettably. By using appendices, the *Annals of the Han Dynasty* successfully solved this problem. In this book, all the events with a known year but unclear dates were listed at the end of that year's events under the title "this year". Even the personages and systems without any clue of time were normally placed under certain years, either at the end or in the middle.

Furthermore, the *Annals of the Han Dynasty* improved the method of combining narration with authorial comments. On the basis of the traditional commentary mode of the annals established by *Zuo's Commentary*, it adopted the new ways of making authorial comments in the *Records of the Historian* and the *Book of the Han Dynasty* with some innovations in the ways of commenting, reasoning, and expression of emotions, which, with its unique style, helped establish the basic framework of the commentary style of the annals. In this book, authorial comments were made in the form of "Xun Yue says", which was more flexible than that in *Zuo's Commentary*. Depending on the specific historical figures or events, the comments ranged from a few dozen words to nearly nine hundred, on some occasions even over one thousand words. They were very persuasive with penetrating analyses and concrete examples punctuated by emotional touches, which added much to its power of influence and won high praises of many latter historians. Fan Ye, the author of the *Book of the Latter Han Dynasty*, for example, praised Xun Yue for his "extremely beautiful discussions". And Li Shimin, Emperor Taizong of the Tang Dynasty, also spoke approvingly of him for his profound comments.

In short, the *Annals of the Han Dynasty* is an important link in the development of the annalistic style of history and a representative work in its mature stage, although it is academically inferior to *Zuo's Commentary*, the *Records of the Historian*, and the *Book of the Han Dynasty*. According to some scholars, if the development of the annals in China could be compared to the climbing of a number of steps, the *Spring and Autumn Annals*, being the first of its kind, would be the first step; *Zuo's Commentary*, which made some improvements in many ways, would be the second step; and the *Annals of the Han Dynasty*, being a mature annalistic history, would be the third step, as it paved the way to the summit of the annalistic style of historiography. This metaphor sounds very appropriate.

The *Spring and Autumn Annals, Zuo's Commentary*, and the *Annals of the Han Dynasty* represented and reflected the continual development and maturation of the annals, which did not stop until the appearance of a new style of historiography, i.e., the chronological-biographical history created by Sima Qian's *Records of the Historian*. Thus, in the following centuries, the annalistic style of history entered a state of slow development and, in the Sui and Tang Dynasties, gradually slumped into a decline. In the Tang Dynasty, in particular, when official historical records were all written in the chronological-biographical style, annalistic histories came to be shelved by historians. The fact the Xun Yue's *Annals of the Han Dynasty* was nearly lost is sufficient evidence. According to *A Bibliography of Canons and Literature* of the *New Book of the Tang Dynasty* by Ouyang Xiu, from the Han Dynasty through the Tang Dynasty, there were published 90 chronological-biographical history books in 4,085 volumes by 70 historians, compared with only 48 annals with 947 volumes written by 40 historians in the same period, less than one fourth of the former in terms of volumes. In sharp contrast to the flourishing of official chronological-biographical history, the annals made no progress either in quantity or in quality, as no monumental works were published in this period. Only a few of them have been included in the bibliographies of history books, such as *Sketchy Annals of the Sui Dynasty, Annals of the Tang Dynasty*, and *Chronicles of the Tang Dynasty*. And as most of them have been lost, it is impossible to know how they were written.

In the Northern Song Dynasty, however, the annals, which began to decline in the two Han Dynasties, experienced some new changes and leapt into a new golden age. The hallmark of this age is *History as a Mirror for Governance* by Sima Guang.

Chapter Two

Sima Guang and
His *History as a Mirror for Governance*

After a period of slow development and decline in the Han and Tang Dynasties, the annalistic style of historiography greeted an age of renaissance in the Song Dynasty when there arose a craze for annals among historians. One apparent fact was that the annalistic style history books far outnumbered the chronological-biographical histories published in this period. According to *A Bibliography of Classics and Books* in the *History of the Song Dynasty*, there were only 57 chronological-biographical history books with 4,473 volumes published in the Song Dynasty, while the number of annals reached 151 with 10,575 volumes, which was just the reverse of what had happened in the Han and Tang Dynasties. The most important factor behind this sharp contrast was the publication of *History as a Mirror for Governance*, a great history book in the annalistic style. This book was a new milestone after the *Records of the Historian* in the development of the historiography in ancient China, for which its author Sima Guang has enjoyed equal fame with Sima Qian. Since then they have been referred to as "the two Simas in the field of historiography".

1. A Biographical Sketch of Sima Guang

Sima Guang (1019–1086), who styled himself Junshi, was born in the Town of Sushui of Xia County in the Prefecture of Shan, which is in today's Shanxi Province. By curious coincidence, right across the Yellow River there was Hancheng County, hometown of the other extraordinary historian Sima Qian.

As a boy, Sima Guang was not only intelligent and diligent, but also brave and resourceful. The story of his breaking an enormous vat filled with water to save another child who had fallen into it made him a household name in China. According to his biography in the *History of the Song Dynasty*, he often attended lectures on *Zuo's Commentary* and explained the main points to his parents back at home when he was only a seven-year-old boy.

In the third lunar month of the fifth year of the Jingyou Period of Emperor Renzong (1058), Sima Guang became a *jinshi* (metropolitan graduate) after passing the highest imperial examination, whereupon he started his political career. At that time the whole dynasty was in a precarious situation as the whole country was beset by rebellions of ethnic minorities and bandits, and natural disasters such as floods and draughts, which impoverished the people and dragged the government into the mire of financial crisis. Naturally, there arose a voice among far-sighted people both inside and outside the government for reform and change in order to rescue the empire. The upper strata of the ruling class also had a heated debate between reformism and conservatism. Sima Guang was not involved in this debate, neither before nor after he began his official career, as he was constantly migrating as a petty local official, far away from the center of the political whirlpool of the capital. Besides, he happened to be on a three-year mourning leave after the death of his father and was thus not drawn into the historical storm when Fan Zhongyan and his followers introduced their new reform policies in the Period of Qingli (1041–1048). However, this does not mean that he was indifferent to what was going on. Ideologically, he was against radical reforms. In his view, it was not necessary to pull a house down as long as it was still habitable. Rather, a little repair work would be good enough. He rejected fundamental changes and accepted only gradual step-by-step reforms. As his ideas were so out of tune with those of the popular officials who called for reform to save the country from social disturbances, it was only too natural that he was not successful in his political career.

For nearly two decades, Sima Guang was transferred from one place to another as a petty official such as administrative assistant. During this period he was never promoted chief local official, neither did he have any outstanding achievements in his work. In other words, he "cut no figure" in this period.

In the third year of the Jiayou Period (1058), Sima Guang was transferred to the capital, first as an administrative assistant at the Prefecture of Kaifeng, then as a supernumerary at the Department of Revenue, and finally he was promoted Edict Attendant and Expositor-in-Waiting of the Hall of Heavenly Manifestations, and a member of the Remonstrance Bureau. "Edict Attendants" were civil officials whose responsibility it was to provide advice to the emperor when he needed it; "Expositor-in-Waiting" was merely a title for scholars who were supposed to lecture on literature and history and work as the emperor's advisors. Even Remonstrance Officials were only supposed to put forward proposals. In the eighth year of the Jiayou Period of Emperor Renzong (1063), when he was forty five years old, Sima Guang was still a Remonstrance Official, without any real power except to submit criticisms and proposals.

It was not until the eighth year of the Jiayou Period (1063) when Emperor Renzong died of illness and Yingzong succeeded to the throne that Sima Guang's political career took an upward turn. Emperor Renzong had had three sons who had all died young. He then had to adopt his nephew Zhao Zongshi as his son, but did not appoint him crown prince. When his health deteriorated, Sima Guang, Prime Minister Han Qi and some other officials strongly advised him to appoint his heir as soon as possible, and thus Zhao Zongshi became the crown prince with a new name Zhao Shu. Upon the death of Emperor Renzong, Zhao Shu succeeded to him and became Emperor Yingzong. As he appreciated both Sima Guang's help and his moral integrity and erudition, he soon promoted him Auxiliary Academician of the Dragon Diagram Hall and Expositor-in-Waiting. With these special royal favors, though they were advisory positions, Sima Guang gained easy access to the emperor. He might have been more successful in his official career if he had had taken advantage of this opportunity. However, being an honest and upright man, he strictly abided by the laws and rules laid down by the founding fathers of the Song Dynasty. When Emperor Yingzong expressed his wish to promote his biological father King Yi of Pu'an, Sima Guang unwisely offended the emperor by strongly arguing against it with the censors Lü Hai and Fan Chunren on the grounds that it violated the traditional rituals. Thus he lost a good opportunity to rise to higher positions, although he was not demoted like the other two.

Frustrated as he was in the political arena, Sima Guang was not demoralized. Instead, he directed his energies to the study of history. In the third year of the Zhiping Period (1066), he completed the eight-volume *Comprehensive Records* and submitted it to Emperor Yingzong. Amazed at his brilliance demonstrated in the book, the emperor immediately ordered him to select some assistants to set up an editing bureau and accomplish the book *Biographies of Emperors and Outstanding Officials in the Past Dynasties* with all necessary reference materials, stationery and even daily necessities for him. All these were new royal graces to Sima Guang.

In the fourth year of the Zhiping Period (1067), Emperor Yingzong died and Emperor Shenzong succeeded to the throne. The intelligent young emperor, seeing that a grave crisis was brewing for the ruling class as the people were being impoverished and the country weakened with each passing day, decided to reform. So Wang Anshi, a determined reformist, was put in an important position. Meanwhile, Sima Guang continued to enjoy royal graces for his profound knowledge. In the ninth lunar month of that year, both of them were promoted Imperial Academicians.

Sima Guang and Wang Anshi had been colleagues for a long time. Academically, they held high esteem for each other, and they could even be close friends when discussing academic matters. When it came to the matter of reform, however, they would immediately drop their friendliness. When he was promoted imperial literary attendant with Wang Anshi, Sima Guang was rather displeased and tried to decline the appointment with the excuse that he was not good at writing parallel prose, but later he was compelled to accept the position as the emperor rejected his excuse. Soon he broke up with Wang when the latter pushed his reform.

In the first year of the Xining Period (1068), there erupted a bitter argument between the two. Because of the serious natural disasters in Hebei Province that year, the government found itself in financial difficulty. At a court meeting over the Southern Suburb Sacrifice to Heaven, Prime Minister Zeng Gongliang proposed that the Emperor stop granting rewards to the officials. Emperor Shenzong then passed this proposal to the Institute of Academicians for discussion. Sima Guang was in favor of the proposal as he held that the act of reducing expenditure for the relief work should start from the court. Wang Anshi, on the other hand, insisted that tapping new resources was more important and that the financial difficulty was due to poor management. This was the first clash between them before the reform movement started as they both refused to compromise.

In the second year of the Xining Period (1069), Emperor Shenzong appointed Vice Premier Wang in charge of the reform. Before long, the Finance Planning Commission was established and the *Law of Young Crops* and other new laws began to be enforced. Refusing to remain silent, Sima Guang submitted many memorials against them. Emperor Shenzong did not adopt his proposals, but he still hoped that they both could work for him. A short time later, Shenzong appointed him Vice Military Affairs Commissioner. To his surprise, the obstinate man insisted that he would rather be a civilian if Wang stayed in such an important position. The other equally obstinate man also made clear to the emperor that he would not accept Sima Guang's promotion as long as he himself was Vice Premier. At first the emperor still tried to make a compromise. He sent a message to Sima Guang that the Privy Council was in charge of military affairs, and that all officials should do their respective duties and should not decline royal appointments with any excuse. However, Sima Guang still refused to work in the same court with Wang Anshi. He insisted that the emperor give him a position outside the capital. In autumn that year, he finally resigned the position of academician of the Duanming Palace and became Prefect of Yongxing (today's Xi'an city in Shaanxi Province). In the following year, when Wang Anshi became Prime Minister, Sima Guang resigned the position as the chief local official and asked for the position of censor-in-chief of the Censorial Bureau of the West Capital in the city of Luoyang, which was a nominal position. Later he served as the supervisor of the Congfu Taoist Temple on the Songshan Mountain for four terms, doing the managing work of the temple. Thus he lived in Luoyang for fifteen years as an idle official for six terms.

When Sima Guang first came to Luoyang, he wrote a poem titled "My Yearning" in which there were two lines: "What is left with me is nothing but innocence; what I have for the wise Emperor is my undivided loyalty." Through such poems he expressed his pride for his innocence and loyalty to the emperor. In this period, he moved the editing bureau to Luoyang and concentrated on the writing of *History as a Mirror for Governance*. He built a house to the north of Superior-men-respecting Lane and named it "Solitary Delight Garden", where he read and wrote his books every day, and sometimes he entertained his friends with poems and wine.

Needless to say, Sima Guang did not stop his activities against Wang Anshi's reform. His close friends such as Fu Bi and Wen Yanbo were all "resigned" officials who were against the reform. Since "birds of a feather flock together", it is not difficult to see that his political attitude never changed. In the meantime, he kept hammering the reform measures in his memorials to the emperor. Even when he contracted a serious disease and had difficulty uttering words in the fifth year of the Yuanfeng Period (1082), he wrote *A Posthumous Memorial* in case he would die, in which he attacked Wang Anshi as "both stupid and obstinate", "disrupting the system established by our ancestors", and "reviving the evil and removing the good, and relinquishing what is right for what is wrong".

In the seventh year of the Yuanfeng Period (1084), Sima Guang completed *History as a Mirror for Governance*, which won him high appreciation of the emperor and the position of Academician of the Government-assisting Hall. In the following spring, Emperor Shenzong passed away and, as the new emperor Zhezong was only ten years old, the real power came into the hands of Grand Empress Dowager Gao, who had always hated the reform movement. Gao immediately appointed Sima

Guang advisor of the imperial secretariat in participation of the imperial administration. In the spring of the first year of the Yuanyou Period (1086), Sima Guang was appointed left vice minister of the Secretariat, and concurrently advisor of the imperial secretariat, and actually became prime minister. Soon the reformists who had followed Wang Anshi were all deposed and conservatives were promoted. Consequently, the new laws and regulations enforced by Wang were abolished and the political situation changed drastically.

Unfortunately, Sima Guang worked as prime minister for only over six months before he died of illness, which put an end to his long political struggle with Wang Anshi. Nevertheless, the struggle between the reformists and conservatives in the Northern Song Dynasty did not pass with him. Actually it became fiercer. In the eighth year of the Yuanyou Period (1093), when Grand Empress Dowager Gao died and Emperor Zhezong assumed power, a number of officials who hated Sima Guang, such as Zhang Dun and Cai Bian, were promoted. And he nearly suffered the misfortune of having his coffin dug out from his grave and his body exposed.

The great philosopher Zhu Xi[1] once passed a judgment on Sima Guang to the effect that he had done one good deed in the fifteen years when he was in Luoyang, that is, the writing of *History as a Mirror for Governance*; and after he came to power, he did one bad deed, that is, the abolition of all the new decrees that had been enforced in the past fifteen to sixteen years, which was disapproved even by conservatives like the poet Su Shi and his father. This judgment sounds reasonable.

It is true that the political struggle with Wang Anshi was an important part of Sima Guang's life and an important basis for any judgment to be passed on him, but we must not forget his greatest contribution, i.e. his book *History as a Mirror for Governance*. Before we can fully understand the book, it is necessary to learn something about his character, scholarly

---

[1] Zhu Xi (1130 – 1200), or Master Zhu, a prominent philosopher, writer and government official of the Southern Song Dynasty. He was the leading figure of the School of Principlism and the most influential rationalist Neo-Confucian in China. He made contributions to Chinese philosophy by assigning special significance to the Confucian Four Books.

attainments, and personal experiences, as well as his political views.

2. The Writing of *History as a Mirror for Governance*

History as a Mirror for Governance is the most systematic and comprehensive general history of the annalistic style ever written in China. This magnum opus consists of two hundred and ninety-four volumes, spanning a long period of one thousand three hundred and sixty-two years, from the twenty-third year of the reign of King Weilie of the Zhou Dynasty (403 B.C.) in the Warring States Period to the sixth year of the Xiande Period of Emperor Shizong of the Later Zhou Dynasty (959), the last of the Five Dynasties. It is the longest span of history covered by any Chinese annals. This great project, which cost Sima Guang nineteen years of painstaking labor, is acknowledged as a magnificent feat in the development of the historiography in China.

It was out of both academic and political reasons that Sima Guang decided to write the book.

Sima Guang had an abiding love for history from his childhood to old age. In his studies, he found a serious lapse — there was not a single concise but complete general history of China, which posed a great difficulty to learners of history. As far back as in the fourth year of the Huangyou Period of Emperor Renzong (1052), before he started the work, he said to his friends that he was considering writing a history book in imitation of Zuo Qiuming's annals and Xun Yue's concise prose style under the guidance of a unique theory embracing various theoretical schools. Being aware that, since no one could possibly read all the 1,500-odd volumes of history books including the *Records of the Historian* and *A History of the Five Dynasties* published in the whole millennium after the appearance of the *Spring and Autumn Annals*, in a few years, people's inclination for simpler things would leave those lengthy books shelved and render them into oblivion, Sima Guang decided to write a new history book that was concise and comprehensive enough to replace the bulky and voluminous histories of the seventeen preceding dynasties.

In the middle period of the Northern Song Dynasty, with the seething popular discontent at home and incessant raids by the tribes of Liao and Xia on the borders, the whole country was on the verge of falling apart. In this situation, there arose an increasingly strong voice for "better governance" both inside and outside the court. Sima Guang, who "deemed history his life's work", decided to provide the rulers of the country with historical lessons by writing a history book which delineated the rise and fall of the past dynasties, and described the joys and sorrows of the people in his discussions of selected historical events. In his "A Memorial for the Submission of *History as a Mirror for Governance*", he asked Emperor Shenzong "to examine the gains and losses of today with reference to the rise and fall of past dynasties, and to remove the evil for the good, and relinquish what is wrong for what is right" for the improvement of the governance and the stability of the country. With the emperors as part of the intended readership, he realized that, for their convenience, the book must be written in the simplest possible form to give prominence to the key points. As there were already seventeen official history books in imitation of Sima Qian's and Ban Gu's styles, most people could not possibly read them all, not to mention the emperors who had to attend to a myriad of affairs every day. Therefore, Sima Guang decided to include only those materials which "bear on the rise and fall of the country and the weal and woe of the common people, and those which are either good enough to be taken as models or bad enough to serve as lessons".

Still another motive of Sima Guang was to attack Wang Anshi's reform movement. It is true that he had developed his idea of writing the book before Wang started the reform movement and that he could not possibly have entertained the motive of thwarting the movement by writing a history book at the very beginning, but it should be noted that the greater part of the book was completed after he declined the position of Vice Military Affairs Commissioner. Of the nineteen years that he devoted to the writing of the book, fifteen were spent in Luoyang when he was a powerless idle official, which happened to be in a period when Wang was presiding over the reform movement. When the movement was first initiated, Sima Guang took the opportunity of expounding history to the emperor and suggested that "our ancestors' laws and regulations should not suffer any change". In support of this opinion, he cited as a precedent the fact that no revision was made to the laws and regulations drafted by Xiao He in the early stage of the Han Dynasty. Later, he kept submitting from Luoyang memorials to Emperor Shenzong bombarding Wang's reform, and his political attitude never changed although his proposals were ignored. In an attempt to persuade the emperor that no reform had ever been successful because they were detrimental to the country and people, he left no stone unturned to establish historical grounds. So when he was working on the book, he made great efforts collecting similar historical cases as evidence against the reform.

As was mentioned above, Sima Guang planned to write a general history of the annalistic style when Emperor Renzong was in power. For this he first wrote a five-volume *Chronicle of Events* which listed the major events from the Warring States to the Five Dynasties Periods as a brief account of the rise of fall of each dynasty. In the first year of the Zhiping Period (1064), he submitted it to Emperor Yingzong. On the basis of this, he wrote the eight-volume *Comprehensive Records* which started from the twenty-third year of the reign of King Weilie of the Zhou Dynasty (403 B.C.) to the third year of the reign of the second emperor of the Qin Dynasty (207 B.C.). Later it became the first eight volumes of *History as a Mirror for Governance*. This book attracted Emperor Yingzong's attention and appreciation, who shortly issued an order for him to set up an editing bureau in the Literature-venerating Institute and granted him special approval to select assistants for the writing of *A Biography of Emperors and Outstanding Officials in the Past Dynasties*. If the writing of *History as a Mirror for Governance* had been his personal effort so far, it now became an official project with special imperial approval. In the fourth year of the Zhiping Period (1067) when Emperor Shenzong succeeded to the throne, Sima Guang expounded his *General Records* to the new emperor, which again won the imperial commendation for its "helpfulness to the governance of the country with the past as a mirror". Later, the emperor gave it a new name *History as a Mirror for Governance*. He even wrote a preface to it himself and encouraged Sima Guang to continue the work. Thus the book was upgraded as an imperial textbook for emperors to draw on others' experiences in the ruling of the people.

History as a Mirror for Governance was an accomplishment of a team of scholars. In the editing bureau under the leadership of Sima Guang, there was a number of employees, including the chief writer, assistant writers, and copiers. The chief writer was naturally Sima Guang himself. The assistant writers included Liu Shu, Liu Ban, and Fan Zuyu[1]. The language reviser of the whole book was Sima Guang's son Sima Kang. This was a capable team of scholars with a common goal. The division of labor among those scholars was very natural as each member excelled in certain academic fields.

Liu Shu, who styled himself Daoyuan, became a *jinshi* at the age of eighteen. An additional examination on Confucian classics established his fame when he amazed the whole capital with a "number one". While his special field was history, he was conversant with almost every branch of learning. As he could talk with equal eloquence on the governance of the country, historical figures, natural sciences such as geography and astrology, and even the histories of many eminent families, he was considered a historical genius of the time. Sima Guang said in admiration of him that he had all the events, big and small alike, in several thousand years at his fingertips. Naturally, Sima Guang immediately thought of Liu Shu when he received the imperial order to select assistants. At the beginning, Liu was in charge of the first draft for the Wei, Jin, and the Northern and Southern Dynasties. After Sima Guang moved to Luoyang, he was also requested to go there for this project, where he undertook the preparation of the first draft for the Five Dynasties. He in fact made more contribution than all the other assistant writers, as he was not only responsible for the two parts mentioned above, but he was also involved in the decision of

---

[1] Fan Zuyu (1041 – 1098), a famous historian of the Northern Song Dynasty. He took part in compiling *History as a Mirror for Governance* and made outstanding achievements in compiling histories of the Tang Dynasty.

the stylistic rules and layout of the whole book. Furthermore, he solved most of the problems which cropped up in the process of the work. Thus he was actually the deputy chief of the whole project. Unfortunately, he died in the first year of the Yuanfeng Period (1078) before the book was completed.

Liu Ban, who styled himself Gongfu, became a *jinshi* in the Qingli Period (1041–1048) and served as a county magistrate and prefect for twenty years. A learned man of letters, he was a renowned expert in the history of the Han Dynasty. He was the author of the four-volume *Corrigenda of A History of the Eastern Han Dynasty*, in which he corrected numerous errors and mistakes in *History of the Latter Han Dynasty*. Besides, he was one of the writers of *Notes on History of the Han Dynasty by Three Liu's*. In the project of *History as a Mirror for Governance*, he was at first in charge of the history of the Han Dynasty and later he took over the part of the Northern and Southern Dynasties unfinished by Liu Shu. However, as he never lived in Luoyang, he could not discuss the project face to face with Sima Guang. After he finished the first draft of his work, he quitted the job.

Fan Zuyu, who styled himself Mengde and Chunfu, was orphaned and adopted at an early age by his grand uncle Fan Zhen who, as a famous scholar on the history of the Tang Dynasty, had participated in the writing of *The New History of the Tang Dynasty* for seventeen years. Under the nurture of his adoptive father, Fan Zuyu also had great attainments in the studies of the Tang Dynasty. Sima Guang, who was a close friend of Fan Zhen, became acquainted with Fan Zuyu as a young man. In the third year of the Xining Period (1070), with the emperor's approval, he selected Fan as a team member in charge of the volume on the Tang Dynasty. After the death of Liu Shu, Fan took over and completed the first draft of the Five Dynasties. He joined the editing bureau later than most of the others, but he worked there longer than all of them. He stayed in Luoyang for fifteen years and worked with Sima Guang until the project was accomplished.

Sima Guang's son Sima Kang, who styled himself Gongxiu, was a well-read scholar with outstanding intelligence. He became the language reviser of the whole book at the age of twenty-nine after the death of Liu Shu and he assisted his father in the following seven years.

Needless to say, *History as a Mirror for Governance* owes much to the collective wisdom and hard work of all the writers but more credit goes to its chief writer Sima Guang. The assistant writers like Liu Shu, Liu Ban, and Fan Zuyu only contributed to the writing of the first draft. All the other work, from the format and style, to the selection and verification of historical materials, to the trimming and polishing of language, was done by himself. In a letter to one of his friends, for instance, he revealed his pains in pruning and finalizing the manuscript: He spent four years revising the first draft of the history of the Tang Dynasty written by Fan Zuyu, which originally consisted of over 600 volumes, at the speed of three days a volume and finally cut it down to 81 volumes. This was a mere example which showed how much pains he took in the whole process. After the completion of the work, he wrote in his *Memorial for Submitting History as a Mirror for Governance* to the emperor, "All my humble energies have been dedicated to this book," which, indeed, was not a self-glorifying statement.

As was mentioned, *History as a Mirror for Governance* was the fruit of collective work as it was beyond the capacity of any single person. However, the contribution of Sima Guang as the coordinator and leader of this team was incomparable with that of any other scholar. It is worth mentioning that he worked out a whole set of methods and procedures from the collection of materials to the finalization of the manuscript, which ensured the smooth and successful implementation of the whole project.

The project was done in three steps. The first step was to make a "table of contents", that is, to arrange all the collected materials chronologically and according to their nature. All the historical materials concerning the events to be recorded were listed under relevant subtitles for selection, since the writers needed to study and classify all the collected materials before they wrote the first draft.

The second step was the writing of the first draft, or the "rough manuscript". The principle of writing this draft was "rather to make it lengthy and tedious than too sketchy". Its purpose was to avoid undesirable omissions and to compare materials from different sources so as to leave ample room for the selection of materials, which also helped the writers to discriminate between true and false stories. The working procedures and contents of the first draft were prescribed by Sima Guang. He made it a rule that the writers must: (a) read all the available materials carefully to be sufficiently familiar with them and to make appropriate classification and arrangement; (b) subject the collected materials to verification and treat different kinds of materials in different ways, with the reliability and truth as the criteria of selection; and (c) make the final selection and arrangement of the materials. He further stipulated that if there were two texts about the same event, the more detailed and clearly expressed one was to be selected; if two texts were complementary to each other, each being more or less detailed than the other in some respects, a new version was to be written to synthesize the materials; in case there were discrepancies in the descriptions of the same event and its dates in two texts, the one which had more supporting evidence or seemed closer to the truth was to be adopted, with the other version included in the notes to show why one was used in preference to the other. As such stipulations were made in advance, the assistant writers were able to coordinate and cooperate in respect of the principles, style, and format when they were writing the individual parts of the book. This laid a solid foundation for the final manuscript and greatly facilitated the work of finalization.

The third step was the finalization of the manuscript. Many historical records show that the "table of contents" and the first draft of the individual parts of *History as a Mirror for Governance* were mostly done by the three assistant writers, while the final deletion of materials, polishing of language, and verification of certain facts for the decision to include or exclude a particular version of a historical event, as well as the writing of the final manuscript, were all done by Sima Guang independently. This was an extremely complicated procedure that required extremely careful and meticulous work, since the success or failure of the whole project hinged on it. It is not difficult to imagine what a challenge it must have been for him to turn the first draft of his three assistants into the final version, which was only one-third of the former in size. After the whole book was completed, two large rooms of the first draft were left unused in his residence in Luoyang.

The finalization of the manuscript consisted not just in the deletion work, but it also involved verification of facts, adjustment of the style and polishing of language. After Sima Guang's painstaking deliberation and masterly touches, the final manuscript of the book was vested with such an integrated style and elegant language that it looked as though it had been done by one person. That ensured the eventual success of the book.

History as a Mirror for Governance was an unprecedented work in the abundance of contents. When talking about the historical materials adopted in the book, Sima Guang's son Sima Kang once revealed that besides official historical records, they made extensive use of a great variety of unofficial histories, genealogies, collected works, and tablet inscriptions. Gao Sisun of the Southern Song Dynasty made a bibliography of two hundred and twenty-six books. In the Qing Dynasty, Hu Yuanchang from the city of Changsha wrote a book *A Research on the Books Cited by History as a Mirror for Governance*, which listed two hundred and seventy-two books under thirteen categories, including official histories, annals, forged histories, miscellaneous histories, records of emperors' activities, anecdotes, records of officials of the past dynasties, miscellaneous biographies, geography books, novels and short stories, categorized reference books, military books, and almanacs. Zhang Xuhou of Huaiyin County of Jiangsu Province made a further study of the book and wrote *A Study of History as a Mirror for Governance* in which he made a list of three hundred and one books under ten categories, including twenty-five official history books, twenty-nine annals, eight genealogies, fifty-four unofficial history books, sixty-seven miscellaneous history books, thirty-five history books of overlords, eighteen biographies, seven books of tablet inscriptions, eight books of memorials to the emperors, sixteen anthologies, ten geography books, fifteen short stories, and nine philosophical books. This number exceeded any previous statistics, but scholars did not stop at that. In the 1980s, Chen Guangchong revised Zhang Xuhou's book. He deleted five books in Zhang's list and added sixty-three, pushing the number up to three hundred and fifty-nine. These statistics, despite their differences, suffice to show the formidable work Sima Guang did over "the mountains of books and seas of documents". One would be lost in wonder at the mere quantity of materials and abundance of contents encompassed in the book.

After the third year of the Zhiping Period (1066) when he received the imperial order to write *History as a Mirror for Governance*, Sima Guang submitted the volumes on each dynasty to the emperor upon their completion. In the following five years before the third year of the Xining Period (1070), when he became the prefect of Yongxing, he finished the parts on the history of the Zhou, Qin, Han and Wei Dynasties in the capital city Kaifeng. In the next fourteen years from the fourth year of the Xining Period (1071), when he moved the editing bureau to Luoyang, to the seventh year of the Yuanfeng Period (1084), he completed the histories of the twelve dynasties from the Jin to Latter Zhou, altogether in two hundred and ninety-four volumes. Thus, the whole project of this historical magnum opus, which covers the history of one thousand three hundred and sixty-two years from the Warring States to the Five Dynasties Periods, was accomplished.

The project of *History as a Mirror for Governance* received close imperial attention from the very beginning. As was mentioned above, Sima Guang won immediate imperial appreciation when he submitted his eight-volume *General Records* to Emperor Yingzong, who then ordered him to establish an editing bureau in the Literature-venerating Institute with assistants selected by himself and provided him with all necessary conveniences, including free access to the Dragon Library and the three institutes of Heavenly Manifestations, i.e. the Institute for the Glorification of Literature, the Academy of Scholarly Worthies and the Historiography Institute, and even stationery and daily necessities. The next emperor Shenzong Zhao Xu showed even greater interest in it. He not only named the book *History as a*

Mirror for Governance and wrote a preface to it personally, but also bestowed on Sima Guang two thousand and four hundred volumes of books which he had collected during his stay in the Prefecture of Ying as the crown prince. He often urged Sima Guang to work harder to complete the book as early as possible, and when the book was finally completed, he appointed him academician of the Administration-assisting Hall.

In the ninth lunar month of the eighth year of the Yuanfeng Period (1085), i.e. one year after the completion of *History as a Mirror for Governance*, Fan Zuyu and Sima Kang were ordered to do another proofreading of the manuscript before it was put into print. They were soon joined by the famous writer Huang Tingjian[①] with the recommendation of Sima Guang. In the tenth lunar month of the following year, the work was finished and the manuscript was sent to the city of Hangzhou to be carved on the printing wood blocks. In the seventh year of the Yuanyou Period (1092), when the printing work was completed, the book was instantly acclaimed as being "equal to the six Confucian classics". Later, for political reasons, Sima Guang himself narrowly escaped the tragedy of having his body dug out from his grave and exposed to the public after his death, and the book was nearly banned, but it eventually survived and has been handed down, and Sima Guang himself also has enjoyed equal honor with Sima Qian as a great historian because of the book.

3. The Characteristics and Value of *History as a Mirror for Governance*

History as a Mirror for Governance has been highly acclaimed by scholars since it was published. Wang Yinglin[②] of the Song Dynasty said that it was unsurpassed by any other book that had ever been printed. This might be a slight exaggeration, but it did reflect the popular opinion then. Undoubtedly,

---

① Huang Tingjian (1045 – 1105), courtesy name Luzhi and style names Shangu Hermit and Fuweng, an artist, poet and scholar-official of the Northern Song Dynasty. Besides his poetry, he was admired for his calligraphy and painting. He was the founder of the Jiangxi Poetic School.
② Wang Yinglin (1223 – 1296), courtesy name Bohou, a historian and scholar-official of the Southern Song Dynasty. He was well-versed in textual research and published works in various fields such as Confucian study, literature, history, and geography. *The Tri-word Primer* is often attributed to him.

this book is the most outstanding history book of the annalistic style with distinctive characteristics and is a landmark of a new stage in ancient Chinese historiography, particularly in the writing of annals.

This book assimilated and developed the inherent merits of the annals published in the previous dynasties and reached the pinnacle of the annalistic style of historiography in ancient China.

Firstly, it set up a scope for the general history in the annalistic style. The form of the general history was created by Sima Qian with his *Records of the Historian*. However, after the publication of the *Chronicles of the Han Dynasty* by Ban Gu and the *Annals of the Han Dynasty* by Xun Yue, most of the chronological-biographical and annalistic histories were dynastic histories. A small number of general histories had been published since the Northern and Southern Dynasties, such as the 620-volume *General History* by Emperor Wudi of the Liang Dynasty in imitation of the *Records of the Historian*, the 270-volume *Records of History by Topics* by Yuan Hui of the Northern Wei Dynasty in imitation of *General History*, and the 300-volume annalistic *General History* by Yao Silian of the Tang Dynasty, but they all withered as quickly as they bloomed because of their poor quality, due to the limitations of the material conditions or the writers' capability. Emperor Wudi's *General History* was mostly destroyed in the suicidal fire by Xiao Yi, i.e. Emperor Yuandi of the Liang Dynasty in Jiangling, and the rest was lost in the Northern Song Dynasty. Yao Silian's *General History* got lost towards the end of the Tang Dynasty. Thus, there was no complete general history in the early years of the Song Dynasty. In the Northern Song Dynasty, there were so many history books that no scholar could possibly read them all. This called for a general history of appropriate size and yet with all the important events and personages through which the reader could perceive the general trend of historical development. Answering this call of the times, Sima Guang devoted all his energies to it for several decades and finally came up with the first complete annalistic general history of China which presented a clear picture of the rise and fall of the dynasties in one thousand three hundred and sixty-two years to the readers and filled a gap in the historical literature of China. Mutually complementary with the *Records of the Historian*, an encyclopedic chronological-biographical history, Sima Guang's book has been applauded as one of "the twin gems in historical literature" in the academic history of ancient China and is recognized as an immortal historical work. Integrating the annalistic style with the form of general history, this book has proved to be far superior to traditional annals and set a new model for the annalistic histories to be written later.

Secondly, just as Zhang Pu[①] of the Ming Dynasty pointed out in his *Preface to the Reprint of History as a Mirror for Governance Topically Arranged*, *History as a Mirror for Governance*, by recording historical events under the years in which they took place, followed the tradition of the annals. Liang Qichao[②] of the Qing Dynasty also remarked in his *Research Methodology in the Studies of Chinese History* that annals mainly followed the years. This time-centered way of recording historical events, which was first established by the *Spring and Autumn Annals* and *Zuo's Commentary*, was further developed by *History as a Mirror for Governance*. In the recording of time, the book absorbed the new developments in the making of astronomical almanacs of that time. In particular, it followed the *Eternal Calendar* by Liu Xisou, an expert in astronomical almanacs in the Northern Song Dynasty, in the determining of the dates of historical events in old historical records. In this way, it eliminated a substantial number of errors and mistakes in this respect. On the basis of the method used in the *Spring and Autumn Annals* and *Zuo's Commentary* which recorded events in the order of date, month, season, and year, another way of "putting the year (or the year of a certain period) under the reign of a certain emperor, which was further put under a certain dynasty" was added in the book in view of its nature as a general history. This in a way reflected the progress of the time and historical studies. As regards those materials with obscure dates, some clear rules were followed in the book: An event without a clear date

---

① Zhang Pu (1602 – 1641), a prolific writer of the late Ming Dynasty. He was the leader of Fushe, a progressive society of that time, and an outspoken critic of the corrupt officials at the imperial court.
② Liang Qichao (1873 – 1929), a journalist, philosopher, and reformist in the late Qing Dynasty, who inspired Chinese scholars with his writings and reform movements. He organized reforms with Kang Youwei in 1898.

was to be put under a certain month; in case the month was unclear, it was to be put under certain year; if the year was also unclear, it was to be appended to a more significant event; and if there was no such an event to which it could be appended, it was to be put under a certain estimated year. In this way, those materials without clear dates were treated appropriately. And in this respect, other annals like *Zuo's Commentary* and the *Annals of the Han Dynasty* seemed to be far inferior to it.

Related to the basic time-centered characteristic of annals, there is another important issue of how the years were to be numbered, as it involved the legitimacy of reigns in the feudal society. After the reign of Emperor Wudi of the Han Dynasty, all the emperors used certain reign titles. When the country was united, the recording of historical events according to their reign titles posed no difficulty since these titles themselves were indicators of time. However, when it came to a period during which the country was split among several governments, each with its own reign title, the use of certain reign title would involve the problem of legitimacy. Before working on the period of the Three Kingdoms when three dynasties, i.e. that of Wei, Shu, and Wu, coexisted, for example, one had to answer the question of whose reign title should be used first. After taking into full account various different opinions, Sima Guang decided on the following principles: First, the dynasties were to be treated "according to the actual contributions they made to history". In other words, whether a dynasty was treated as the central government or a local state depended on its contribution, and there was no question of legitimate or illegitimate government. The Zhou, Qin, Han, Jin, Sui, and Tang Dynasties had all united the whole country and were therefore treated as dynasties set up by Sons of Heaven, and those dynasties which had never controlled the whole country were treated as states. Second, those states which existed when the whole country was split were treated in the light of the preceding or following dynasties, which showed sufficient respect to the continuity of history without honoring one and slighting others. Since the Han Dynasty was followed by the Wei Dynasty, which in turn was succeeded to by the Jin Dynasty, which was passed on to the Song and Chen Dynasties in the division between the North and South and later conquered by the Sui Dynasty, and since the Tang Dynasty was passed on to the Song Dynasty through the Liang and Zhou Dynasties, the problem of dating the historical events which had taken place when the country was divided found a solution. Although these principles have been challenged by some scholars who fear that the use of the reign title of one state without referring to those of others in a period of division would cause confusion and inconvenience, we cannot but see that they are reasonable principles that have demonstrated the insight of Sima Guang, since they help keep both the truth and the continuity of history.

Thirdly, *History as a Mirror for Governance* inherited and developed the patterns of authorial comments on historical events. As was mentioned above, the form of authorial comments was first established in *Zuo's Commentary* in which the author discussed historical events through the mouths of authorities and quotations from classical works, or through direct comments introduced by the clause "a superior man may say". Nevertheless, the scope of such comments was rather narrow, limited only to the issue of "rituals". In the *Annals of the Han Dynasty*, the discussions were expanded to include political gains and losses, but they seemed to be too lengthy and pedantic. In *History as a Mirror for Governance*, this tradition of making authorial comments was further developed, and such "historical criticisms" became an organic part of the whole book, scattered in relevant discussions on individual events. They were presented either as Sima Guang's personal comments in the form of "His Majesty's humble subject Sima Guang says", or as the sayings of certain renowned scholars or celebrities in the previous dynasties in the form of "somebody said". According to statistics, there were two hundred and eighteen such "comments", of which one hundred and nineteen were Sima Guang's personal comments. These historical criticisms expressed the authors' thoughts and feelings about the malpractice of the time, particularly about the positive and negative experiences in the governance of the country in the preceding dynasties with profound insinuations. Through objective revelations and discussions of the virtues and evils of the emperors in the past, he pointed out that emperors must restrain themselves as governing a country was like "standing on the brink of an abyss, or treading on thin ice", where extreme caution was imperative. His purpose in writing and discussing history in this way was presumably to provide a mirror of the past for the emperors, since discussions of the merits and demerits of ancient monarchs could "trace the rise and fall of the past dynasties and help the existing monarchs draw lessons from them". Historians in the feudal times held two opposing attitudes regarding the writing of history: One was avoiding the taboos of those who were in power and who were along the same political line with the authors, exaggerating their merits and covering up their demerits, or purposely smearing the images of their political enemies; the other was sticking to facts, neither concealing the evils nor exaggerating the virtues of anyone in order to present a truthful picture of history for people to draw lessons from. Sima Guang's attitude was obviously of the latter type. His book represented or, so to speak, painted a fairly truthful picture of history for people of latter periods. That accounts for the reason why it is considered by some scholars a relatively credible political history of China.

Fourthly, the verification of the historical events by Sima Guang vested ancient annals with a new look. When he was writing about a particular event, he would refer to several different records. Thus he would inevitably face the challenge of various versions of the same event, some of which might be false. The verification of the stories, therefore, was extremely important. In this respect, Sima Guang was actually preceded by Pei Songzhi[1] who had written *Annotations on Records of the Three Kingdoms*, in which he cited many different versions of the events as a supplement to the *Records of the Three Kingdoms*[2] by Chen Shou[3]. Pei Songzhi did

---

[1] Pei Songzhi (372 – 451), courtesy name Shiqi, a historian and government official of the late Eastern Jin Dynasty. He is best known for making annotations to *Records of the Three Kingdoms* (*Sanguozhi*) written by Chen Shou in the 3rd century.

[2] *Records of the Three Kingdoms* (*Sanguozhi*) is a history work which covers the late Eastern Han Dynasty (circa 184–220) and the Three Kingdoms period (220–280). It provided the basis for the 14th-century historical novel *Romance of the Three Kingdoms*.

[3] Chen Shou (233–297), courtesy name Chengzuo, an official and writer who lived during the Three Kingdoms period and the Jin Dynasty.

this mainly "to provide more sources of reference", while Sima Guang's purpose in doing so was "to reach the truth through comparison". Pei Songzhi's methods were in essence the collection and preservation of historical materials, which was a new way of making notes on books; Sima Guang's approach, on the other hand, made the writing of history a branch of science by eliminating the false and retaining the true historical materials. It was thus obvious that there was a leap in quality from Pei Songzhi's "providing more sources of reference" to Sima Guang's "reaching the truth through comparison". *History as a Mirror for Governance* took its materials mainly from seventeen official chronological-biographical history books. As those books used historical figures as the key line, one and the same event might be described in different places, and each version might contradict the others. In Sima Guang's book, each event had only one version. Besides official histories, there were many kinds of unofficial histories, in which there were serious distortions and self-contradictory points. After a careful study of all these, Sima Guang clarified numerous facts and corrected many mistakes, which greatly enhanced the credibility of the historical materials in the book. Qian Daxin[1], a well-known scholar in the Qing Dynasty, said, "One cannot read the seventeen histories without referring to *History as a Mirror for Governance*, for it corrected many mistakes in various history books, including unofficial histories, from which it took the materials. Just as some ancient scholars commented, the book recorded more events in less space than all the previous books." This comment, indeed, is pertinent.

Another important innovation of Sima Guang was the thirty-volume *A Study of Different Versions of Historical Events* which he wrote as an appendage to *History as a Mirror for Governance*. A number of scholars before him had made certain research on different versions of historical records, but they had either relied on their own judgment as to which version

---

[1] Qian Daxin (1728 – 1804), courtesy name Xiaozheng and style name Xinmei, a scholar-official, historian, and linguist of the Qing Dynasty, often considered one of the best Chinese scholars in the 18th century. He advocated Han Confucianism and criticized the Song and Ming approaches of Confucian studies.

should be adopted, or simply piled the materials together for readers to decide what to believe when they found contradictory historical materials mixed with both true and false versions. No special efforts had ever been made to verify the historical materials, still less to write a special book on it. Sima Guang did both. He not only studied the materials carefully and adopted those which were more reliable, but also wrote a special book about it in order to preserve those unselected materials for future reference. This had at least three merits: (a) the cited unofficial materials were all verified by him, which naturally enhanced their credibility; (b) the materials that were noted "unverified" or "a possible version" in the book provided room for later scholars to do further research; and (c) as it gave readers a complete picture of how the author "reached the truth through comparison", readers did not have to take the trouble to repeat the same comparisons if they were done correctly. It was thus an extremely valuable book which could not have been written by a less upright or over self-confident scholar. In a comment on this book, the *General Catalogue of the Complete Library of Four Treasuries* points out, "Sima Guang was the first historian to write a book on why he selected certain materials in preference to others in his work." This is sufficient affirmation of his serious attitude towards the study of history.

Fifthly, Sima Guang's contribution to the traditional style of annals also lies in the fact that he set a precedent for the writing of a series of books in illustration of an important book. During or shortly after the completion of *History as a Mirror for Governance*, he published a number of books which were mutually complementary with it and formed an organic whole with it. These books included the five-volume *Chronicles of Historical Events*, the one-volume *Guide to the Use of History as a Mirror for Governance*, the thirty-volume *A Study of Different Versions of Historical Events in History as a Mirror for Governance*, the thirty-volume *Table of Contents of History as a Mirror for Governance*, the eighty-volume *The Key Events in History as a Mirror for Governance*, and the sixty-volume *An Abridged Edition of History as a Mirror for Governance*.

Two of these books, i.e. *A Study of Different Versions of Historical Events in*

History as a Mirror for Governance, and *Table of Contents for History as a Mirror for Governance*, were submitted to the emperor together with *History as a Mirror for Governance* itself. The importance of these two books in his eyes was thus easily imaginable. As the former has already been discussed, we shall just have a brief discussion of the latter.

Compared with the seventeen histories published before, *History as a Mirror for Governance* was much shorter, but it still had two hundred and ninety-four volumes with over three million words. Sima Guang noted that only one scholar named Wang Shengzhi had managed to read the whole book, and that all the other people would quit after reading a couple of volumes. This was not because the language was too obscure, but because the book was still too lengthy and required too much time and energy to read the whole of it. Moreover, although it was written in chronological order, it was still difficult to locate the relevant discussions of an event. This was taken into consideration when Sima Guang was working on *History as a Mirror for Governance*, which explains why the two books were published together. However, although like all other books, the *Table of Contents for History as a Mirror for Governance* had a table of contents with a number of unique characteristics, it was written in the form of a chronicle table, in which the record of each event was divided into three parts, i.e. the year when the event took place, which was placed on the top line, the volume number of the book where the event was recorded, which was placed on the bottom line, and a brief description of the event, which was placed in the middle. Thus, the "table of contents" was actually an abridged version of the whole book. It provided an index for all the important events that took place each year with subtitles for the convenience of readers. This effort of Sima Guang for readers's convenience in addition to all the energies he spent on the writing of the book was in itself an indication of his exceptional conscientiousness as a historian.

In terms of the styles of books today, *Chronicles of Historical Events* could be regarded as a chronicle table and outline of *History as a Mirror for Governance*, while *Guide to the Use of History as a Mirror for Governance* could serve as a guide to the use of the book; *A Study of Different Versions of Historical Events in History as a Mirror for Governance* was a series of annotations on the book as well as its supplement; the *Table of Contents for History as a Mirror for Governance* was its index and abstract, and the *Key Events in History as a Mirror for Governance* and the *Abridged Edition of History as a Mirror for Governance* were naturally its simplified and abridged versions respectively. These books were both self-contained and mutually complementary to one another. This great creation in the writing of history books exerted a far-reaching influence on later historians.

Furthermore, the immortality of *History as a Mirror for Governance* also lies in the fact that it assimilated and developed the merits of both the annalistic and chronological-biographical styles of historiography and thus formed its unique style.

The development of culture has always been the result of the mutual influence, assimilation, and complementation of various factors. Despite their respective characteristics, chronological-biographical histories and annals are not completely opposite to each other. Sima Qian, inherited and assimilated the tradition of annals. A typical example was the chronicles of emperors in his *Records of the Historian*, which were directly adapted from annals. Starting from this book, all the chronicles of emperors in official histories were predominantly written in the annalistic style. This shows that the mutual influence or assimilation between the annalistic and chronological-biographical styles of historiography was not only possible, but it had a precedent to go by.

From Sima Qian's *Records of the Historian* to Sima Guang's *History as a Mirror for Governance*, the chronological-biographical style of historiography experienced over one thousand years of development and reached a high degree of maturity. In an age like the Song Dynasty when historical studies flourished, it was only too natural that a conscientious historian like Sima Guang, who had developed a keen interest in history since his childhood, had studied official chronological-biographical histories such as the *Records of the Historian* and *Chronicles of the Han Dynasty* seriously and thus had a deep understanding of both the merits and shortcomings of the chronological-biographical style of historiography. This was undoubtedly the essential prerequisite to the adoption of the strong points of the chronological-biographical history.

If we read *History as a Mirror for Governance* in comparison with the *Records of the Historian*, we will easily find that the former assimilated the strong point of the chronological-biographical history in putting historical figures at the center, and applied this method effectively in the light of the characteristics of annals. Specifically, it did the following:

(A) It focused on the deeds of historical figures. Instead of describing one thing for each person as in the biographies of chronological-biographical histories, it tended to piece the deeds of each personage together. Its account of Tian Dan's deeds, for instance, was much more vivid and complete than that in the *Records of the Historian*. For example, it put Tian Dan under the year 297 B.C. and described how he successfully escaped from Anping by wrapping the chariot axles with iron when the city was attacked by the State of Yan, how he helped the State of Qi defend the city of Jimo by playing the trick of sowing distrust between the Yan general Yue Yi and his sovereign, and using every means possible to weaken the morale of the Yan army and boost that of the Qi army, and how he defeated the enemy with the peculiar battle array of bulls on fire in the end. In this way, it succeeded in bringing out the complete image of Tian Dan vividly.

(B) It placed several stories of one and the same personage under different dates, thus facilitating the chronological recording of the events without destroying the completeness of the stories. Lian Po and Lin Xiangru, for example, were known mainly for three stories, i.e. the stories of "Returning the Jade Intact to the State of Zhao", "the Meeting at Mianchi", and "the Union of the General and the Grand Councilor". These were all self-contained but related stories. In this book, they were put under the years 283 B.C. and 279 B.C. respectively in order to keep the stories intact. This way of recording events separately was a creation based on the strong point of chronological-biographical histories in describing the deeds of people with some modifications in accordance with the requirements of annals.

(C) It presented complete images of historical figures with supplementary descriptions where necessary. In this book, there was often a short biographical sketch after the death of certain person, which supplied additional information about his deeds and thus helped paint a complete picture of the man. For example, after mentioning the death of the Grand Preceptor Feng Dao in the fourth lunar month of the first year of the Xiande Period of Emperor Taizu of the Later Zhou Dynasty (954), it added a sketch of his life and works with the author's comments, which helped painting a vivid picture of the cunning and unctuous old official. This extensively used method in the whole book was obviously also borrowed from chronological-biographical histories.

(D) It depicted the characters of historical figures with their own words. This method, was borrowed by Sima Guang from Sima Qian's *Records of the Historian*. Under the item of the eleventh lunar month of the twenty-fourth year of the Jian'an Period of Emperor Xiandi of the Han Dynasty (218A.D.), for example, it delineated the character of Sun Quan, particularly his ability of placing the right person in the right post and his tolerance of his officials' shortcomings through his own dialogues with others. The actual words of the historical figures added much to the vividness of the language of the book and undoubtedly helped avoid the dullness of the day-to-day accounts of events in annals.

Besides, this book assimilated and integrated into its account of historical events certain anecdotes, memorials of some famous officials to emperors, folk rhymes, and proverbs, which were often used in chronological-biographical histories in describing historical figures. This further enhanced the vividness of descriptions of the characters.

In short, *History as a Mirror for Governance* pushed the annalistic style of historiography to a new height by combining the strong points of annals with those of chronological-biographical histories. Apparently superior to all the annals that had appeared before it, the book was an extraordinary contribution to the development of the annalistic history and even the whole historiography in ancient China. The famous scholar Hu Yinglin of the Ming Dynasty once observed, "The annalistic history reached its pinnacle in Sima Guang's book. Its publication instantly rendered all the annals that had appeared before the Song Dynasty obsolete." A slight exaggeration as it is, it allows us to recognize the universally acknowledged indelible contribution of Sima Guang to Chinese historiography. Thanks to the appearance of this book, the annalistic style of history, which had suffered a serious decline, restored its glory. Besides, it inspired a number of new styles of history, such as the event-focus style and outline-focus style, and gave Chinese historiography a new look.

Chapter Three

History as a Mirror for Governance and History-Mirrorology

Upon its publication, *History as a Mirror for Governance* instantly won the unanimous acclaim of the academic circles. In the Southern Song Dynasty, even the chieftain of the Nüzhen ethnic group, who was the emperor of the Jin Dynasty in the north, could not conceal his respect for the book when he bestowed a set of it on his crown prince. In the nine centuries since its completion in the seventh year of the Yuanfeng Period (1084), this book has been reprinted so many times that it has become an extremely popular historical work. It is estimated that it has been reprinted seventy-six times in the past nine hundred years, that is, it has had a reprint every thirteen years on an average. This is rare for ancient Chinese history books, which itself indicates how much social attention it has received. What is worth noting here is the fact that it has attracted generations of scholars devoted to the study of it, including the writing of sequels, annotations, errata, and simplified versions, or even rewriting it in other styles. All these efforts eventuated in the birth of a branch of learning with the book itself as its object of study, i.e. history-mirrorology, which endured through the ages as an influential branch of historiography in the later stages of ancient China.

The term history-mirrorology was coined by Hu Sanxing[1] in his

---

[1] Hu Sanxing (1230 – 1302), courtesy names Shenzhi, Meijian and Jingcan, a historian in the late Song Dynasty to the early Yuan Dynasty. He wrote valuable corrections and commentaries on *History as a Mirror for Governance*.

Preface to An Analysis of the Mistakes in History as a Mirror for Governance. However, as concepts are always preceded by facts, the study of the book had actually started among Sima Guang and his assistants long before Hu Sanxing put forward this term.

The earliest works of history-mirrorology were those mentioned above, including Sima Guang's *Study of Different Versions of Historical Events in History as a Mirror for Governance, A Table of Contents for History as a Mirror for Governance, the Key Events in History as a Mirror for Governance,* and *An Abridged Edition of History as a Mirror for Governance.* These books, which were all out of Sima Guang's own hands on *History as a Mirror for Governance,* facilitated the comprehension of the book and helped reveal its aim and style.

In general, all the studies of the book, including its annotations, adaptations, imitations, sequels, textual researches, enlarged editions, and criticisms, can be considered within the scope of history-mirrorology. Some scholars divided it into four categories, i.e. the compilation of sequels, annotations, textual researches and supplements, and criticisms. The two classifications are essentially the same, differing only in whether or not to include a particular study into a certain category. In view of the fact that some adaptations of *History as a Mirror for Governance* were recognized as new styles of history, such as the event-focus style and outline-focus style of history, which exerted a profound influence on the general development of historiography after the Song Dynasty, it is necessary to discuss them in a separate section. Here our discussion shall be confined to the compilation of sequels, annotations, textual researches and supplements, and criticisms. This should not give rise to misunderstanding, for our purpose is not to attract attention with novelty, but to exclude adaptations from history-mirrorology.

1. The Sequels of *History as a Mirror for Governance*

The sequels of *History as a Mirror for Governance* refer to those historical records written as its continuations in imitation of its format but with materials collected by the writers themselves. As this book does not cover remote ages before King Weilie of the Zhou Dynasty and the contemporary Song Dynasty when the authors were alive, it naturally failed to include some historical periods in ancient China. So it occurred to some scholars to write sequels to the book in imitation of its style. Such sequels can be divided into two types, i.e. "pre-sequels" and "post-sequels" which recorded historical events that took place before and after those covered in the book respectively.

The first one who thought of implementing this idea was Liu Shu, who assisted Sima Guang in the compilation of *History as a Mirror for Governance*.

At the very start of the compilation work, Liu Shu advised Sima Guang to start the book from earlier ages such as the times of Emperors Yao and Shun. Sima Guang, however, dismissed the idea with the argument that one must not go beyond the line drawn by Kong zi. Liu Shu, who considered this an undesirable blemish of the book, decided to do it himself. Besides, he thought that the history of the one hundred and eight years under the reigns of the first five emperors of the "current dynasty" (i.e. the Song Dynasty) should also be recorded. He planned to write two books called *A Pre-sequel to History as a Mirror for Governance* and *A Post-sequel to History as a Mirror for Governance* respectively. Unfortunately, in the ninth year of the Xining Period (1076), he was paralyzed and was confined to bed for nearly two years as the result of a family misfortune. Unable to fulfill his ambition, he canceled the plan for the second book and renamed the finished "pre-sequel" *An Unofficial Sequel to History as a Mirror for Governance*. The book consisted of ten volumes, including the one-volume *Chronicles of the Age since King Fuxi*, one-volume *Chronicles of the Xia and Shang Dynasties*, and the eight-volume *Chronicles of the Zhou Dynasty*. This was the first sequel to *History as a Mirror for Governance*.

The idea of writing sequels to *History as a Mirror for Governance* had, as a matter of fact, brewed in Sima Guang's own mind for a long time. The *Chronicles of Historical Events*, which he submitted to the emperor in the first year of the Zhiping Period of Emperor Yingzong (1064), for example, spanned over one thousand and eight hundred years from the Gonghe Period (841–826 B.C.), which was over four hundred years before the starting point of *History as a Mirror for Governance*, to the Epoch of Five Dynasties. In the second year of the Xining Period of Emperor Shenzong (1069), he suggested that a table of officialdom system be written in the style of the *Book of the Han Dynasty* to record the historical changes of the bureaucratic establishment of the Song Dynasty. After he was granted the imperial permission, he spent twelve years writing the ten-volume *Chronicles of the Bureaucratic Establishment* in collaboration with others, which covers the period from the end of the Xiande Period (959) of the Later Zhou Dynasty to the Xining Period (1068) of Emperor Shenzong of the Song Dynasty. His original intention to record the entire history of China from remote ages to his own day could thus be easily perceived from these two books. According to *A Study of the Classics and Ancient Books*, Sima Guang and Liu Shu had agreed to collaborate on *A Post-sequel to History as a Mirror for Governance* based on official histories and with additional information from other sources. Due to the early death of Liu Shu and busy administration work of Sima Guang himself, this wish was not fulfilled, but Sima Guang still managed to finish the sixteen-volume *Notes on the History of the Song Dynasty by a Man from the Su River* which recorded various events of different sources from the time of Emperor Taizu to Emperor Shenzong of the Song Dynasty. According to Ji Yun, author of *An Annotated List of the Complete Library of Four Branches of Books*, this book was part of the preparation for the writing of the planned *Post-sequel to History as a Mirror for Governance*. From this it could be inferred that the *Post-sequel to History as a Mirror for Governance* would have been written if it had not been for the early death of Liu Shu and Sima Guang.

Fortunately, this wish of Sima Guang was fulfilled by other people. In the tenth year of the Chunxi Period of the Southern Song Dynasty (1183), the outstanding historian Li Tao[1], after forty years of hard work,

---

[1] Li Tao (1115 – 1184), courtesy name Renfu or Zizhen, a historian and scholar-official of the Southern Song Dynasty. He devoted four decades of his life compiling *The Draft of a Sequel to History as a Mirror for Governance*, a history work on the Northern Song Dynasty (960 – 1127).

published *the Draft of a Sequel to History as a Mirror for Governance*[①], which was recognized as the best of all the sequels to the book. An intelligent and diligent scholar in historical studies, Li Tao was known for his exceptionally profound knowledge about the anecdotes of the Song Dynasty. He first started working on the history of the reign of Emperor Taizu in Sichuan Province without the commission of the court, but he gradually attracted royal attention with his extraordinary achievements, a total of about fifty books, including *the Draft of a Sequel to History as a Mirror for Governance* which cost him nearly his whole lifetime.

According to Li Tao himself, the working principles of his book and even the arrangement and order were all borrowed from Sima Guang. This was true. For example, the basic principle of his book, i.e. "rather making it too detailed than too brief", was stipulated by Sima Guang in one of his letters to Fan Zuyu. Following Sima Guang, Li Tao also applied the method of "reaching the truth through comparison". In the notes of his book, he gave the fullest possible explanations of all the materials, including those obscure historical records, regarding their sources, differences, reliability, and the reasons why one version was adopted in preference to others, so that readers could not only see why he selected certain materials instead of others, but also judge the correctness of his selections. This was itself a basic principle of Sima Guang in the compilation of the *Study of Different Versions of Historical Events*. Even the word "draft" in the title of his book was borrowed from an earlier unpublished version of Sima Guang's book. All this shows that Li Tao's book was a faithful imitation of that of Sima Guang both in name and in the working principles. The profound influence of *History as a Mirror for Governance* on it was thus self-evident.

The Draft of a Sequel to History as a Mirror for Governance boasted an abundance of source materials, including the archives of the Song government, original documents, unofficial histories, and varieties of collected works of many authors. It recorded the historical events under

---

① *The Draft of a Sequel to History as a Mirror for Governance*, published in 1183, chronicles the history of the Northern Song Dynasty (960 – 1127). Unfortunately, only 520 of its 980 chapters are extant.

the reigns of the nine emperors of the Northern Song Dynasty from Emperor Taizu to Emperor Qinzong. Originally, it consisted of nine hundred and eighty volumes, but those about the reigns of Emperors Shenzong, Zhezong, Huizong, and Qinzong were not carved and printed later, and even those about the other five reigns had become scarcely available by the Qing Dynasty. The existing version of this book was copied from *the Yongle Great Encyclopaedia* by the editors of the *Complete Library of Four Treasuries*, in which the historical records about the reigns of Emperors Huizong and Qinzong, as well as parts of those about the reigns of Emperors Yingzong, Shenzong, and Zhezong, were missing. Despite all this, it remains the most complete history of the Northern Song Dynasty ever written. Besides, it connects *History as a Mirror for Governance* so closely in time that the two look like sister books — it starts from the first year of the Jianlong Period (960) when Emperor Taizu came to the throne, immediately following the year where *History as a Mirror for Governance* ends — the sixth year of the Xiande Period of the Later Zhou Dynasty (959). The wish of Sima Guang and Liu Shu was thus fulfilled by Li Tao. And the profound influence of *History as a Mirror for Governance* on the development of historiography found a first successful demonstration in *the Draft of a Sequel to History as a Mirror for Governance.*

Following Li Tao, another scholar of the Southern Song Dynasty named Li Xinchuan[1] wrote the two-hundred-volume *Chronicles of Events Since the Jianyan Period*[2], which recorded the history of the thirty-six-year reign of Emperor Gaozong from the first year of the Jianyan Period (1127) to the thirty-second year of the Shaoxing Period (1162), which immediately followed the time covered by Li Tao's book. It should be noted that this book was also an imitation of *History as a Mirror for Governance*, whose influence was pervasive in the book. Li Xinchuan attached great importance to the textual research of historical materials, and his method

---

[1] Li Xinchuan (1166 – 1243), courtesy name Weizhi or Bowei and style name Xiuyan, a historian and official of the Southern Song Dynasty.

[2] *Chronicles of Events Since the Jianyan Period* offers a detailed historical account of the period 1127 – 1162. It was written on the basis of a wide collection of records and narratives in official histories.

basically consisted in referring to as many books as possible, eliminating the false and retaining the true, and adopting the best version in the book. He adhered to the principle of rejecting all hearsay materials, intentionally adorned materials, and documents of obscure sources, which reflected the serious attitude of a real scholar. Like Sima Guang, he took great pains to achieve the conciseness of language, so that "the book was lengthy but not tedious, and its discussions were varied without being confusing", and historical events were presented coherently and vividly. *A Synoptic Catalogue of the Complete Library of Four Treasuries* commented, "Li Tao imitated Sima Guang but proved to be slightly inferior, while Li Xinchuan imitated and surpassed Li Tao." This appraisal is not just strong commendation of Li Xinchuan, but it draws a clear line of succession from Sima Guang to Li Tao and Li Xinchuan.

Under the influence of Sima Guang's *History as a Mirror for Governance*, the annals became the most popular style of historiography in the Song Dynasty. Besides such influential works as Li Tao's and Li Xinchuan's books mentioned above, there appeared a number of other sequels to Sima Guang's book, including the fifteen-volume *Chronicles of the Resurgence of the Song Dynasty-a Sequel to History as a Mirror for Governance* by Liu Shiju, which recorded the historical events after Emperor Gaozong moved the capital to the city of Hangzhou, from the first year of the Jianyan Period (1127) to the seventeenth year of the Jiading Period of Emperor Ningzong (1224), and the eighteen-volume *Pre-sequel to History as a Mirror for Governance* by Jin Lüxiang, which was also an imitation of the book based on Liu Shu's *Unofficial Sequel to History as a Mirror for Governance*. It starts from Emperor Yao of Tang (2356 B.C.) of the Legendary Period, and ends at where Sima Guang's book starts. Although they were hardly comparable to those of Li Tao and Li Xinchuan, these books, to some degree, reflected the attraction of Sima Guang's book to the people then.

Even in the Ming and Qing Dynasties, the charm and influence of *History as a Mirror for Governance* did not wane despite the passage of time. Many historians of these two dynasties still cherished an unflagging enthusiasm for the history of the Song and Yuan Dynasties along the lines of Sima Guang.

Under the reign of Emperor Jiajing of the Ming Dynasty (1522–1566), two metropolitan graduates, Xue Yingqi and Wang Zongmu, wrote two books with the same title *History of the Song and Yuan Dynasties: a Sequel to History as a Mirror for Governance*, which consisted of one hundred and fifty seven and sixty four volumes respectively. These two namesake books were intended to record the history of the Song and Yuan Dynasties along the lines of Sima Guang, but they were dismissed by scholars as laughing-stocks for their scanty and even false information.

In the Qing Dynasty, two scholars, Xu Qianxue and Bi Yuan[1], compiled a one-hundred-and-eighty-four-volume *Reedition of Sequels to History as a Mirror for Governance* and a two-hundred-and-twenty-volume *Sequel to History as a Mirror for Governance*[2] respectively. Xu's book starts from the first year of the Jianlong Period of Emperor Taizu of the Song Dynasty (960) and ends at the twenty-seventh year of the Zhizheng Period of Emperor Shundi of the Yuan Dynasty (1367). It was based on Wang's and Xue's books but was much more informative and of much better quality. Its layout, in particular, was an exact copy of *History as a Mirror for Governance*. Besides the text, it contained numerous notes on different versions of the historical events for the convenience of readers and even authorial comments in the form of "His Majesty's humble subject Qianxue says". However, due to the author's lack of sufficient academic competence and his mistakes in the selection of materials, as well as due to the inaccessibility of many historical records, the book failed to serve as an ideal sequel to Sima Guang's book since it did not contain extensive verified information.

Bi Yuan's *Sequel to History as a Mirror for Governance*, on the other hand, was considered the most influential annalistic sequel to Sima Guang's book. His success was attributable to various factors. First, many historians

---

[1] Bi Yuan (1730 – 1797), courtesy name Xiangheng or Qiufan, a historian and poet of the Qing Dynasty.

[2] *Sequel to History as a Mirror for Governance* chronicles the rise and fall of the four dynasties Song, Liao, Jin and Yuan in 960 – 1368. It mainly follows the model of *History as a Mirror for Governance*.

in the Ming and Qing Dynasties had a common wish to write an annalistic history of the Song and Yuan Dynasties along the lines of Sima Guang. A fairly large number of scholars before Bi Yuan had devoted themselves to this work but failed to achieve satisfactory results. One of the most important reasons was the difficulty in the collection of materials. Under the reign of Emperor Qianlong (1736–1795), with the publication of *A Synoptic Catalogue of the Complete Library of Four Treasuries*, many books that had been difficult to come by became easily accessible. The objective conditions for Bi Yuan's work were thus incomparable with those for Xu Qianxue and his predecessors. Besides, Bi Yuan enjoyed the help of a number of distinguished historians such as Zhang Xuecheng[1], Shao Jinhan[2], and Qian Daxin when he was working on the draft. Shao Jinhan and Qian Daxin even checked its layout and did the proofreading before the final manuscript was completed. In the whole process, the book was revised four times. Therefore, it was actually the fruit of the collaboration of a group of highly renowned scholars.

The *Sequel to History as a Mirror for Governance* starts from where the *History as a Mirror for Governance* ends, i.e. the beginning of the Song Dynasty, and ends at the last year of the Yuan Dynasty. This book overcomes the main drawback of those sequels of Sima Guang's book published before it which were basically mechanical combinations of the annals of the Song Dynasty and those of the Yuan Dynasty. With the histories of the Song, Liao, Jin, and Yuan Dynasties merged into an organic whole, it is a real, and, indeed the best annalistic history of the period from the Song Dynasty through the Yuan Dynasty. No wonder Fan Xizeng said in his *Answers to Frequently Asked Questions about Important Books — a Revised Edition*, "With the publication of this book, the numerous sequels by all the other scholars of the Song, Yuan, and Ming Dynasties can now be relegated to the wastepaper basket." This was very true. In fact, not long after the

---

[1] Zhang Xuecheng (1738 – 1801), courtesy name Shizhai and style name Shaoyan, a historian, writer and philosopher of the Qing Dynasty. He has a famous saying, "The six classics are all history."

[2] Shao Jinhan (1743 – 1796), courtesy name Yutong and style name Eryun or Nanjiang, a historian of the Qing Dynasty. He was in charge of compiling the history section of *The Complete Library of Four Treasuries*.

publication of this book, the scholarly enthusiasm for writing annals of the Song and Yuan Dynasties along the lines of the *History as a Mirror for Governance* was suddenly dampened, and then the historians turned their eyes to the history of the Ming Dynasty, which followed the Yuan Dynasty. Thus we had the sixty-volume *Chronicles of the Ming Dynasty* by Chen He and the one-hundred-volume *History of the Ming Dynasty as a Mirror for Governance* by Xia Xie.

Chen He lived in the Periods of Emperors Qianlong and Jiaqing (1796–1820). He became a *jinshi*, in the years of Emperor Jiaqing and was once secretary to the minister of the Ministry of Works. His *Chronicles of the Ming Dynasty* records the history of the Ming Dynasty along the lines of Sima Guguang. Starting from the deeds of Emperor Hongwu (1368–1398) through the years of the last three princes of the Dynasty, the book was extremely strict about the selection of materials. He died when he was working on the fifty-second volume, and the rest eight volumes were finished by his grandson Chen Kejia. Under the reign of Emperor Tongzhi (1862–1874), when he was the Imperial Inspector of Jiangsu Province, Ding Richang expressed his wish to publish a history of the Ming Dynasty after the appearance of Bi Yuan's *Sequel to History as a Mirror for Governance*. Yu Yue then recommended him to take Chen He's *Chronicles of the Ming Dynasty* as a continuation of the book since they were of the same style. Ding gladly adopted his suggestion, and thus the *Chronicles of the Ming Dynasty* was published under official patronage.

In comparison, Xia Xie was less lucky. His book was not well-received, despite his academic family background and the abundance of historical materials in it, whose references included not only such official histories as *True Records of the Ming Dynasty*, *True Records of the Qing Dynasty*, and the *History of the Ming Dynasty*, but also various kinds of unofficial histories and anthologies which, to some extent, supplemented the *History of the Ming Dynasty*. The support of Ding Richang for Chen He's *Chronicles of the Ming Dynasty* pushed it further into the shadow. In fact, it had only a lithographic edition printed in the years of Emperor Tongzhi. Nevertheless, it remains one of the most readable sequels of *History as a*

Mirror for Governance because it preserved abundant materials about the Ming Dynasty and corrected many errors and mistakes through a study of different versions of historical events.

After *History of the Ming Dynasty as a Mirror for Governance*, there was no sequel to Sima Guang's book in the same style, but there were two annalistic works on the history of the Qing Dynasty — two namesake books called *the Records of the East Flowery Country* written by Jiang Liangji and Wang Xianqian respectively. Jiang's book consists of thirty-two volumes, starting from the beginning of the Qing Dynasty and ending at the thirteenth year of the reign of Emperor Yongzheng (1735), while Wang's book was based on Jiang's book but he supplemented it with the historical materials about the reigns of Emperors Qianlong, Jiaqing, Daoguang (1821–1850), Xianfeng (1851–1861) and Tongzhi. The final edition of the book consists of six hundred and twenty-five volumes known as *the Records of the East Flower Country in the Reigns of Eleven Emperors*. Strictly speaking, however, they were no more than a barely tolerable tail to *History as a Mirror for Governance* since they were only a draft of an annalistic history of the Qing Dynasty with its materials copied mainly from the *True Records of the Qing Dynasty.*

The review of the sequels to *History as a Mirror for Governance* above reveals an apparent fact: It set the pattern for the annalistic history, so that the annalistic histories which appeared in the Song, Yuan, Ming, and Qing Dynasties, almost without exception, borrowed its name and followed its principles. This alone was sufficient evidence of its lofty status in the eye of the people and its profound influence on later historians. That accounts for the comment of some scholars: *History as a Mirror for Governance* is an unprecedented book in the past and an indispensable model for later historians.

2. The Annotations of *History as a Mirror for Governance*

It is a tradition of ancient Chinese historiography to provide annotations for famous history books, and they, too, made tremendous contributions to the original works. For Sima Qian's *Records of the Historian*, there is *the*

Collected Annotations of the Records of the Historian, the *Correct Meanings of the Records of the Historian* by Zhang Shoujie, and *the Collected Expositions of the Records of the Historian* by Pei Yin; for Ban Gu's *the Book of the Han Dynasty*, there is *the Annotations of the Book of the Han Dynasty* by Yan Shigu; for Fan Ye's *the Book of the Later Han Dynasty*, there is Li Xian's *the Annotations of the Book of the Later Han Dynasty*; and for Chen Shou's *the Records of the Three Kingdoms*, there is also *the Annotations of the Records of the Three Kingdoms* by Pei Songzhi.

History as a Mirror for Governance, being a magnum opus that records important historical events and describes relevant systems and institutions, is not easy to understand without annotations. Therefore, soon after its publication, many scholars started to write annotations for the book in imitation of the way annotations had been made for "the first four history books" i.e. *Records of the Historian, Book of the Han Dynasty, Book of the Later Han Dynasty* and *Records of the Three Kingdoms*.

Liu Anshi of the Nothern Song Dynasty was the first scholar who had annotated *History as a Mirror for Governance*. He was a civil official in charge of proofreading when the book was sent to Hangzhou for block printing, and was thus the first person to see the book besides the writers themselves. Taking advantage of this convenience, Liu Anshi wrote a book *the Sounds and Meanings* in ten volumes which, unfortunately, has got lost, but judging from its title, it should be the annotations of sounds and meanings for Sima Guang's book.

Another annotator of *History as a Mirror for Governance* after Liu Anshi was Shi Zhao, who was a native of Sichuan Province, born towards the end of the Yuanyou Period (1086–1094) of the Northern Song Dynasty and died in the reign of Emperor Xiaozong (1163–1189) of the Southern Song Dynasty. He completed *the Annotations of History as a Mirror for Governance* in thirty volumes in ten years, mainly for meanings of words and phonetic notations. This book was not highly evaluated for its carelessness and ignorance.

Besides Shi Zhao's book, there were two popular annotations of *Expositions of History as a Mirror* by Sima Kang and *the Pronunciation of Words in History as a Mirror* by a man named Fei of the Shu Prefecture at the end of the Southern Song Dynasty. The former one was a fake in the name of Sima Kang as the "Haining edition" for it was carved at Haining Prefectural House, and the latter was called Dragon-claw *History as a Mirror*. According to Hu Sanxing's investigation, these two editions were made by people hired by some private publishers, and they were all copied from the annotations by Shi Zhao. Their poor quality is thus easy to imagine.

It seems easy but actually very difficult to provide annotations for history books, for a truly qualified annotator must have, besides a profound knowledge of the ancient pronunciations and meanings of Chinese characters, and the evolution of systems and institutions of different historical periods, and a good understanding of the merits and demerits of the book under annotation, as well as the ability to find and correct the errors and mistakes in it. Shi Zhao, who fell short of such qualifications, naturally made a laughing stock of himself for his poor annotations of the book.

The most outstanding and influential scholar in the annotation of *History as a Mirror for Governance* was undoubtedly Hu Sanxing at the turn of the Song and Yuan Dynasties. Hu was a native of Ninghai County of Taizhou Prefecture with two style names Jingshen and Shengzhi. He became a *jinshi* at the age of twenty-seven in the fourth year of the Baoyou Period in the Southern Song Dynasty (1256) after passing an imperial examination together with some well-known historical figures such as Wen Tianxiang, Lu Xiufu, Xie Bingde, etc. Before the Southern Song Dynasty was conquered by Yuan, when he was an official under Jia Sidao, he advocated resistance against the Yuan Army, but Jia Sidao ignored him. Hu Sanxing developed a keen interest in *History as a Mirror for Governance* at an early age, and he always carried the book with him and consulted experts whenever he met them as he was working at his official posts in various places. He annotated *History as a Mirror for Governance* twice. He first imitated the layout of *Annotations of the Classics* by Lu Deming of the Tang Dynasty and wrote *the Comprehensive Annotations of History as a Mirror for Governance* in ninety-seven volumes and criticisms in ten volumes. Unfortunately, in the second year of the Deyou Period (1276) when the Yuan army took over Lin'an City, he lost all the manuscripts in the turbulence in his escape to Xinchang. It was a heavy blow to him, but he did not give up. After the fall of the Southern Song Dynasty, he returned to his hometown and lived a reclusive life dedicating all his energies to the annotations of *History as a Mirror for Governance*. He bought some other editions of the book, adopted a new layout, and distributed the *Study of Different Versions of History as a Mirror for Governance* and his annotations in different parts of the text of *History as a Mirror for Governance*. He kept working for many years and finally completed *the Pronunciation and Annotations of History as a Mirror for Governance* in the winter of the twenty-second year of the Zhiyuan Period (1285), which was already ten years after the fall of the Song Dynasty. Then he wrote another book *Expositions and Corrections of History as a Mirror for Governance*. After that he started the revision work, which lasted for thirty years. In short, Hu Sanxing made an outstanding contribution to Chinese historiography through the result of his independent work, i.e. the two books — *the Pronunciation and Annotations of History as a Mirror for Governance* in two hundred and ninety-four volumes and *Expositions and Corrections of History as a Mirror for Governance* in twelve volumes.

Hu Sanxing's annotations include: 1) pronunciations of Chinese characters; 2) systems and institutions; 3) names of places; 4) names of persons; and 5) clothing and vessels. His detailed annotations, which were made according to ancient books, greatly facilitated the reading and understanding *History as a Mirror for Governance*.

Compared with those of previous scholars, Hu Sanxing's annotations had a number of apparent merits.

First, his annotations contained cross references for the same events mentioned in different places of *History as a Mirror for Governance*. As an annalistic history, this book normally mentioned a historical event or personage under several years, which made it difficult for readers to get a clear picture of the whole process of the event or all the activities of an important figure. In his annotations, Hu endeavored to compensate for such imperfections for the convenience of readers. For instance, in the one hundred and eighty-eighth volume of the book, which recorded how Du Caigan, a subordinate of Li Mi, killed Bing Yuanzhen for his revenge, Hu Sanxing annotated: "Refer to the 180th volume for the item the ninth lunar month of the first year for Yuanzhen's betrayal of Li Mi." Such annotations, which are pervasive in his books, were of great benefit to the readers. As for important figures in turbulent times such as the periods of the Three Kingdoms, the Sixteen Dynasties, the Northern and Southern Dynasties, the Five Dynasties and Ten States, Hu Sanxing made it a rule to make a note at the first appearance of relevant figures in order to attract readers' attention. For instance, in the eightieth volume of *History as a Mirror for Governance*, which recorded the stories of Liu Yuan in his teens, he noted "the beginning of Liu Yuan's story"; in the eighty-sixth volume, which recorded how Shi Le got his name, he noted "the beginning of Shi Le's story". This has been recognized as the best way in annotating the annalistic history books.

Second, Hu Sanxing's annotations were more than mere notes. In fact he also did sort of proofreading, for he corrected numerous errors and mistakes in *History as a Mirror for Governance*. The methods of his proofreading and annotations appear more in judgments of "proofreading according to the principles" based on theories and professional knowledge; next are judgments of "proofreading in comparison and contrast with other relevant books"; few are the judgments of "proofreading the text itself" and "proofreading in comparison and contrast with ancient books". Besides, he pointed out a large number of errors and mistakes in other scholars' annotations of the book. In this way he set a good example of serious scholarly attitude for later generations.

Third, what distinguished Hu's annotations from those of previous scholars most clearly was not only his detailed annotations, but his pithy and profound comments which normally consisted of a few short sentences, and sometimes only one word. Such comments revealed his passionate patriotic enthusiasm and the lessons he had drawn from the rise and fall of the preceding dynasties. In a sense they were the most important part of the annotations made by a man living in a time of grave national crisis when his country was facing the immediate danger of subjugation by the Yuan army.

In short, Hu Sanxing's annotating work on *History as a Mirror for Governance* was a significant event. His annotations were composed of nearly three million words, almost as long as the original book itself. Covering an extensive range of subjects, these annotations greatly facilitated readers' understanding of the book. Besides, they supplemented a great quantity of historical materials, some of which were no less important than *History as a Mirror for Governance* for the study of the book itself. It is thus no exaggeration to say that Hu's annotations paralleled the book in their contribution to historical studies since we cannot read the book without referring to his annotations. Here we see a solitary man who, in a desolate place and under deplorable living conditions, kept working on this book for three solid decades without ever thinking of fame or fortune. He was really a great man for his contribution not only to the study of *History as a Mirror for Governance*, but also to the development of Chinese historiography.

Hu Sanxing's *Annotations of History as a Mirror for Governance* was published towards the end of the Yuan Dynasty, but it did not attract much attention until the Qing Dynasty when textual study became a prevailing scholarly subject. Then some people began to publish their studies of *History as a Mirror for Governance* annotated by Hu as they admired his expertise in geography and textual study. Many of such books made attempts to correct his mistakes, including, for example, *Corrections of Hu's Annotations of History as a Mirror* by Chen Jingyun in ten volumes, only one of which still exists with sixty three entries, mostly about geographical problems. There were also Qian Daxin's *Corrections of the Annotations of History as a Mirror* in two volumes with over one hundred forty entries, mainly about the geographical and language problems, and *Discussion about the Annotations of History as a Mirror* by Zhao Shaozu, which consisted of over eight hundred entries.

These works, however, targeted at Hu Sanxing's mistakes. No one had ever paid attention to and explored Hu's intention and achievements in annotating *History as a Mirror for Governance*. It was not until the 1940s, when the famous historian Chen Yuan published his *A Tentative Study of Hu Sanxing's Annotations of History as a Mirror for Governance*, that his patriotism and scholarly achievements received due recognition.

Chen's book consisted of twenty chapters, with the first ten chapters on the methodology of historiographical studies and the second ten on historical events. Being the result of the author's three-odd years' intensive study of Hu's over-six-million-word *Annotations*, this book was a fairly comprehensive analysis of it. Its clear writing format of shows: in the first line the original text of *History as a Mirror for Governance* is set flush; in the second line, Hu's annotations are indented with the number of volume of *History as a Mirror for Governance* marked; in the third line, the authorial comments are further indented. With a clear, well-designed format, the book cited over seven hundred and fifty quotations from Hu's *Annotations*, and over two hundred books besides official histories. Hu Sanxing's thought, knowledge and the value of his annotations were thus given due evaluation.

3. Corrections and Supplements of *History as a Mirror for Governance*

Like any other book, *History as a Mirror for Governance*, despite its enormous scope and profound thought, was not immune to errors and mistakes. Sima Guang himself admitted in his memorial to the emperor upon the completion of the book, "I cannot guarantee that the book is free from contradictions and mistakes as the work has lasted for such a long time from the beginning of the Zhiping Period to its completion today." This is not just a modest expression. After the publication of the book, there was no lack of scholars who raised queries about it and corrected its mistakes.

The first scholar to point out some of the flaws in *History as a Mirror for Governance* was Liu Xizhong of the Northern Song Dynasty, who was the eldest son of Liu Shu, Sima Guang's major assistant. Although he had never met Sima Guang, he gained a lot of information from his father about the compilation work on the basis of which he wrote *Queries on History as a Mirror for Governance* in six volumes. With only over six thousand words, the whole book recorded some of the discussions between Liu Shu and Sima Guang on the compilation work with an appendix, i.e. a letter from Liu Xizhong to Fan Zuyu. In the letter, which included a list of eight questions regarding the shortcomings of the book, Liu seemingly consulted Fan, but in fact raised queries about it.

As it was already near the end of the Northern Song Dynasty when *History as a Mirror for Governance* was completed, there was little time left for an in-depth study of this great historiographical work in this dynasty except for Liu Xizhong's *Queries on History as a Mirror for Governance*.

The situation took a favorable turn in the Southern Song Dynasty when there arose a great passion among the scholars for the study of the book. In addition to the making of sequels and annotations, many scholars began to correct the errors in the book and raised queries on it. For instance, in his *Miscellaneous Notes from the Tolerant Study*[1], Hong Mai[2] pointed out the illogical use of the titles of years of events which were named after, rather than before or when they took place, and the over-detailed descriptions of minority ethnic groups in the Jin and Song Dynasties which were irrelevant to the governance of the country. Another scholar Wang Yinglin, who was known for *A Comprehensive Interpretation of Geography in History as a Mirror for Governance*, wrote another book *Record of Observances from Arduous Studies*[3] in two volumes with eleven entries on *History as a Mirror for Governance*, which analyzed its losses and gains. Still another scholar Hu Yin (styled as Zhitang) also pointed out in his *My Humble Opinions on Reading History* the "possible mistakes" in the titles of years and months due to the fact that "the materials selected from the Tang to the Five Dynasties were somewhat contradictory to one another",

---

[1] *Miscellaneous Notes from the Tolerant Study*, a collection of the author Hong Mai's notes on Confucian classics, literature, history, calendar, etc.

[2] Hong Mai (1123 – 1202), courtesy name Jinglu and style name Yechu or Rongzhai, a statesman, Confucian scholar and writer of the Southern Song Dynasty.

[3] *Record of Observances from Arduous Studies*, a dissertation by Wang Yinglin (1223 – 1296) on Confucian classics, astrology, geography, history, and literary criticism.

because of Sima Guang's hastiness in completing the book.

In the Yuan and Ming Dynasties, when the status of *History as a Mirror for Governance* was much lower, the passion for the study of the book also waned. Despite that, however, there was still a number of scholars who engaged in the study of the book, including, for example, Yan Yan and his disciple Tan Yunhou at the turn of the Ming and Qing Dynasties, who were known for their co-authored book *Supplements to History as a Mirror for Governance* in two hundred and ninety-four volumes, on which they spent thirty long years of hard work.

Yan Yan, styled Yongsi, a native of Jiading County of Jiangsu Province, was a *xiucai*, i.e. a scholar who passed the county-level imperial examination in the reign of Emperor Wanli (1573–1620) of the Ming Dynasty. A poor but diligent scholar, he never became an official in his life, but he was said to begin to study *History as a Mirror for Governance* at forty-one, but he was so absorbed in it that he was often found poring over it all day long, forgetting all about eating and sleeping, as he was totally immersed in this vast sea of knowledge. Gradually, however, he began to see some of the errors of omission and contradiction in the book and thus decided to write a book to supplement it. He had a student named Tan Yunhou, who shared his inspirations. They studied the book together every day. According to Yan's own records, they often continued to have discussions over a cup of wine while eating the peanuts they bought from a small local shop after a whole day's hard work.

Tan Yunhou wrote in his *Postscript to the Supplements to History as a Mirror for Governance*, "Historians are liable to commit seven kinds of mistakes, i.e. errors of omission, redundancy, wrong ordering of materials, incoherence, misunderstanding of events, prejudice and misrepresentation. Great as it is, *History as a Mirror for Governance* is not immune to them." Yan Yan also said in the Preface, "The seven kinds of mistakes mentioned in the *Postscript* are really common occurrences." Thus we see that both the teacher and student saw the seven kinds of mistakes in the book and thought it necessary to do the work of correction and supplementation.

In their efforts to correct the seven kinds of mistakes in the book,

Yan and Tan added twenty-four types of work, including rectifying the orthodox dynasties, reserving the declining dynasties, supplementing the titles of years, correcting mistakes, straightening out the disorders, sorting out the jumbled materials, deleting repetitions, and repudiating forges and wrongs, etc. Obviously, they include both correction of errors and supplementation. When explaining why the title of the book did not have the word "correction", Yan Yan said, "For the sacred books of our wise ancestors, any addition or deletion is a sin. The most we can do is supplementation of facts. How dare we 'correct' their books?"

Yan Yan's book was as much praised as it was blamed. Qian Daxin, for example, admired it and said that its contribution to *History as a Mirror for Governance* was second to none except the book by Hu Sanxing." Wang Yingkui, on the other hand, dismissed it as undesirable augmentation of Sima Guang's book and said that what Yan Yan supplemented might be just what Sima Guang had deleted.

Objectively speaking, Yan Yan and his student were the most outstanding scholars devoted to the study of *History as a Mirror for Governance* after Hu Sanxing's time. He discovered a number of flaws in the book, some of which were very serious. It might also be worth mentioning that his book consisted of two hundred and ninety-four volumes, exactly the same as Sima Guang's and Hu Sanxing's books. This coincidence itself is ample manifestation of his goal. Therefore, his book is a useful guide to the study of *History as a Mirror for Governance.*

Admittedly, Yan's book had some obvious weaknesses. The most obvious one was its lengthiness due to over-supplementation of extensive materials cited from a large number of history books, which made the reading of the book a tedious task. Besides, while Sima Guang used over two hundred history books, Yan used only books about the history of seventeen dynasties and periods. In view of this, later scholars made some efforts to make up for these shortcomings. Zhang Dunren, a scholar in the Qing Dynasty, for instance, wrote *A Summary of Supplements to History as a Mirror*, which reduced Yan's book to the size of a pamphlet.

Besides, there were some other influential books by a number of scholars of the Yuan Dynasty such as *Quiet Talks from Zhanyuan* by Bai Ting, *Supplements to History from Jing Studio* by Li Ye, *Talks on Study from Old Shu Studio* by Sheng Ruzi, *Essentials of the Seventeen Histories* by Hu Yigui, and *A Brief Analysis of History as a Mirror for Governance* by He Zhong, etc. These books, being basically reflective notes on Sima Guang's book with considerable insights, also contributed to the development of history-mirrorology.

4. Criticisms on *History as a Mirror for Governance*

Sima Guang's *History as a Mirror for Governance* followed the tradition of historical criticism established by *Zuo's Commentary* and *the Chronicles of the Han Dynasty*. It made a special effort to integrate argumentative discourse with narrative discourse, including both comments of historians in previous times and those of his own with a view to providing a mirror of the past for the governance of the present and the future. This gave ample room for him to air his own views in the book.

Of all the critical works on *History as a Mirror for Governance*, the most important one is probably *On History as a Mirror for Governance*[1] by Wang Fuzhi[2] at the turn of the Ming and Qing Dynasties. However, before we discuss his book, it is necessary to point out that reflective criticism of Sima Guang's book was not initiated by him. As early as in the Southern Song Dynasty, Zhang Shi selected commonly cited authorial comments from the book and edited them into a book titled *Sincere Comments from History as a Mirror for Governance* in three volumes. Li Tao wrote *Comprehensive Reflections on the Six Dynasties in History as a Mirror for Governance* in ten volumes based on Sima Guang's comments on the wars in the Period of Three Kingdoms and the Six Dynasties as a reflection on the moving of

---

[1] *On History as a Mirror for Governance* is a work of historical comments by Wang Fuzhi. It tries to analyze the reasons behind the rise and fall of the different dynasties, evaluate the gains and losses, and comment on important historical figures on the basis of the historical facts in *History as a Mirror for Governance*.

[2] Wang Fuzhi (1619 – 1692), courtesy name Ernong and style name Chuanshan, a philosopher of the late Ming Dynasty to the early Qing Dynasty. He wrote on many topics, including metaphysics, epistemology, moral philosophy, poetry, and politics.

Song's capital to Hangzhou. It was this book that initiated the reflective criticism of *History as a Mirror for Governance*. Towards the end of the Ming Dynasty, Zhang Pu, leader of Fu Society, wrote a book *Comments on the Past Dynasties* in two hundred and thirty-nine chapters using all the chapter titles in *History as a Mirror for Governance Topically Arranged* by Yuan Shu, which covered all the topics in Sima Guang's book. Nevertheless, none of these can be counted as monographs on *History as a Mirror for Governance*. The only book that deserves the name of a genuine monograph is the one by Wang Fuzhi.

Wang Fuzhi, who styled himself Ernong, also known as Jiangzhai, was a native of Hengyang. He was called Mr. Boat Mountain because he spent his last years as a hermit at the foot of Stone Boat Mountain on the east side of the Zheng River in western Hunan Province. Born into a scholarly family and living in a time of internal disturbance and external threat, he gradually developed a keen interest in the practical knowledge of geography, economy, and development of systems and institutions. He took the imperial examinations at the provincial level twice and failed two times. Then he resolved to study for the governance and benefit of the people. After the Ming Dynasty was replaced by the Qing Dynasty, he joined in armed struggles against the Qing government, which ended in failure. Realizing the irreversibility of the political situation, he decided to spend the rest of his life as a hermit at the foot of Stone Boat Mountain, where he wrote his longest and most representative book *On History as a Mirror for Governance*, which is an extremely important work of historical criticism in Chinese historiography.

Generally, the thoughts of historians in the past were reflections of the social realities of their times, which were either intended as advice to the emperors or unintentional revelations of their own ideas. The same was true of Sima Guang, and Wang Fuzhi. Their intentions in the writing of their books, however, were not exactly the same as Wang was still in great sorrow over the fall of the Ming Dynasty. On the one hand, Sima Guang declared that his purpose of writing *History as a Mirror for Governance* was "to examine the gains and losses of the reality of the current dynasty with the rise and fall of the past dynasties as a mirror, to encourage what is good and discourage what is evil, and advise the people to adhere to what is right and stay away from what is wrong". On the other hand, Wang Fuzhi expressed his idea in his book that "both the gains and losses of the past dynasties can be used as mirrors," and what should be done was "to examine the reasons behind the gains and losses and explore the ways to duplicate the gains and avoid the losses." He emphasized that "History should not be used just like a mirror hanging in an empty room." In other words, he was not contented with "encouraging what is good and discouraging what is evil, and advising the people to adhere to what is right and stay away from what is wrong". In fact, he was more concerned with the reasons and causes of the gains and losses in the past dynasties. All this made his analyses more profound and comprehensive than those of Sima Guang.

On History as a Mirror for Governance analyzed and evaluated historical events and figures in the chronological order of the past dynasties with the intention of expounding the author's political views and historical philosophy through his comments. Wang Fuzhi said that the most precious value of history lay in its lessons of the past for the benefit of the future. In his own words, it was "telling stories of the past history as good lessons for future generations". His comment on historical events in the book, rather than empty talk, were serious discussions on their causes and effects, often scintillating with original ideas never expressed by people before and different from those of his contemporaries. The fact that he lived in a time and circumstances quite different from those of Sima Guang enabled him to look at things from the perspective of national interests without any personal prejudice. In his own words, he was "unbiased in the study of what actually happened in history." Thanks to all this, he surpassed Sima Guang in the evaluation of historical events and figures. His remarks often hit home and demonstrated his unique insights when he corrected Sima Guang's biases and other shortcomings. We could probably get more insights and inspirations if we compared his comments with those of Sima Guang's beginning with "Your Majesty's humble subject Guang says" in *History as a Mirror for Governance*. It is, therefore, not an exaggeration to conclude that *On History as a Mirror for Governance* is an important reference book for the study of *History as a Mirror for Governance*.

The sequels, annotations, corrections and supplements, and criticisms of *History as a Mirror for Governance* discussed above clearly indicated the profound and far-reaching influence of this book on the historiography of the later ages. On the other hand, those books discussed above draw a picture of the emergence and development of "history-mirrorology", which kept pushing ahead the studies of this book when the annalistic style of history was at a standstill.

It is worth mentioning that during the period between the 1911 Revolution to the founding of the People's Republic of China in 1949 there appeared a number of comprehensive summary books in the field of history-mirrorology, the most prominent of which were *A Study of History as a Mirror for Governance* by Cui Wanqiu and *History-Mirrorology* by Zhang Xu.

Published in 1934, *A Study of History as a Mirror for Governance* by Cui Wanqiu was the first summary work about history-mirrorology. It consists of twelve sections, encompassing all relevant aspects of the book such as the author's life experiences, his motives in writing the book, the whole working process, the co-authors, its sister books, its source materials, its influence, and others scholars' comments and criticisms. It is basically an introductory work with sporadic comments of the writer himself. Its most valuable part was the section titled "Source Materials" of Sima Guang's book, which gave a list of two hundred and seventy-two books mentioned in *A Study of Different Versions of Historical Events in History as a Mirror for Governance* in the order of citation. Despite some arguable points, Cui's book is still a valuable reference for the study of the source materials of *History as a Mirror for Governance*.

In comparison, Zhang Xu's *History-Mirrorology* is a more comprehensive summative work with a number of unique features. Styled as Xuhou, Zhang Xu was a native of Huaiyin County of Jiangsu Province. He was a teacher as well as an expert in historiography. His book was first published in 1948. He planned to publish a second edition with some supplements in ten years but his wish was not fulfilled until 1981. To date it is still the only comprehensive study and introduction of *History as a Mirror for Governance*. The whole book is divided into seven chapters, including a review of the history of the annals, an introduction to the process of the compilation work, its source materials, the historical criticisms of the book, its methodology and format, its branches and sequels, and its gains and losses, as well as the reformation of the annals. The book is by far superior to *A Study of History as a Mirror for Governance* by Cui Wanqiu in the selection of materials and the checking of historical events. As a most exhaustive review of previous studies on *History as a Mirror for Governance* with a system of its own, it is a basic textbook of history-mirrorology and a must for researchers of *History as a Mirror for Governance*. In the chapter "Gains and Losses of *History as a Mirror for Governance* and the Reformation of the Annals", Zhang Xu concludes that the book has three gains, i.e. the integration of biographies of historical figures with authorial comments, that of textual research with the authors' analysis and personal judgement, and that of historiography with literature; and three losses, i.e. the excessive uniformity of the way in which the years of events are arranged, the over-simplification of cultural historical materials, and the personal prejudices of the authors. Considering the three gains and three losses, he makes a insightful proposal for the reformation of the annals.

In the over six decades since the founding of the People's Republic of China, the study of *History as a Mirror for Governance* has continued to thrive, and numerous monographs and articles have been published on it. On the basis of the existing literature, many scholars have been doing further studies on the annotations, textual studies, and evaluation, as well as the writing process of the book. All this testifies to the fact that Sima Guang's book is a brilliant magnum opus with a far-reaching influence on Chinese historiography. His contribution to its development will not fade out with the passage of time.

Chapter Four

History as a Mirror for Governance and New Styles of Historiography

Liu Zhiji, a historian of the Tang Dynasty, pointed out in the chapter titled Six Styles in his *Generalities on History*, "Many stylistic changes have taken place in historiography since ancient times. There has never been a constant style." These words tell us that ancient Chinese historical works were varied both in form and style, which were changing all the time. In this process of change, we can observe the mutual influence and infiltration of various styles of historiography which often begot new styles while promoting the development and maturation of the old ones, since the maturity of anything itself often means the beginning of its decay. From this perspective, we can see that *History as a Mirror for Governance*, while pushing the annalistic style of historiography to its zenith, gave rise to various factors that were to break through this style itself. A case in point was the emergence of two new styles, i.e. history presented in separate accounts of important events or event-focused style[①] and general outline of history or outline-focused style[②], as a result of scholarly efforts to modify and improve it.

[①] History presented in separate accounts of important events, or event-focused style, began with the publication of *History as a Mirror for Governance Topically Arranged* by Yuan Shu (1131 – 1205).

[②] General outline of history, or outline-focused style, is notably represented by *A General Outline of History as a Mirror for Governance* compiled by Zhu Xi in imitation of *The Spring and Autumn Annals* and *Zuo's Commentary*.

1. *History as a Mirror for Governance* and Histories in the Event-focused Style of Important Events

The earliest style of Chinese historiography was the early annals represented by *the Spring and Autumn Annals* and *Zuo's Commentary*, which were popular in the pre-Qin periods. Such annalistic works recorded history in chronological order with the apparent merits of terseness and conciseness. However, it also had the obvious drawback of incoherence, which seriously disrupted the continuity in the accounting of historical events. An event was often cut into numerous fragments by different dates and, consequently, "one event might span several volumes, which inevitably blurred and distorted the whole picture." In view of this, Sima Qian assimilated the merits and discarded the demerits of the annals and created the style of chronological-biographical history, i.e. history presented in chronicles and biographies, which was to prevail in the Western Han Dynasty. Just as Zhao Yi, a scholar of the Qing Dynasty said, Sima Qian established a number of norms for the writing of official histories from which no one has ever been able to deviate. Following these norms but with some modifications, Ban Gu wrote the first dynastic history in the chronological-biographical style, i.e. *Book of the Han Dynasty*. Since then all "official histories" have been written with these two books as models.

However, this does not mean that the chronological-biographical history was perfect. In point of the fact, it had its inherent deficiencies since its focus was on historical figures. While it was comprehensive enough to give due consideration to time, events and relevant personages by virtue of biographies of emperors and other historical figures, tables of events and records of systems and institutions, it had the obvious defect of redundancy and incoherence, as "an event was sometimes repeated in several sections, which often blurred the picture."

After the chronological-biographical history dominated Chinese historiography for over one thousand years since the Han Dynasty, the annalistic style of historiography regained currency with the publication of *History as a Mirror for Governance* by Sima Guang. This, however, was not a simple return to the starting point, but rather a new development. Living in the Northern Song Dynasty, an age over one thousand years after the creation of the chronological-biographical history, an extraordinary historian like Sima Guang must have had a thorough knowledge about the methodology of this style of history. Therefore, his book could not possibly be a simple return to the style of early annals without borrowing anything from the chronological-biographical history. In fact it enriched the annalistic style by assimilating some of the merits of the latter, such as the use of biographies in the recording of the deeds of important historical figures. This change in recording historical events pushed the ancient annalistic style of historiography to a new height.

Nevertheless, this book was not able to overcome the fundamental defects of discontinuity and inconvenient retrieval of information in annals. With the development of historiography, the new style of history presented in separate accounts of important events finally emerged in the Southern Song Dynasty with the publication of *History as a Mirror for Governance Topically Arranged*[1] by Yuan Shu[2].

It is generally acknowledged that Yuan Shu's book was the first major history book presented in separate accounts of important events. It should be mentioned, however, as early as in the Tang Dynasty, Liu Zhiji had already pointed out, in his comparative study of the annals and chronological-biographical history, that the latter had both the merit of keeping the details of historical events and the demerits of discontinuity and redundancy since one and the same event might be repeated in several sections. On the other hand, the annals excelled in focusing on events experienced by different people in different places without having to repeat them, but in case the events in question had lasted for several years, they still had to be tackled in several volumes, thus blurring the whole picture. This was an example of the scholarly efforts to examine and overcome

---

[1] *History as a Mirror for Governance Topically Arranged* by Yuan Shu, though practically a copy of *History as a Mirror for Governance*, offered an innovative arrangement and therefore became influential in the Ming and Qing dynasties.

[2] Yuan Shu (1131 – 1205), a historian in the Southern Song Dynasty.

the defects of the chronological-biographical history and annals before Yuan Shu wrote his book. Actually, even before Liu Zhiji made theoretical criticisms of the two styles of historiography, explorations had already been made for a style that could keep the virtues of both. Cui Hong of the Northern Wei Dynasty, for example, was said to have written a book titled *Records of Historical Events* which was a general history from remote ages through the Jin Dynasty with a focus on the events. The book, which is lost, seemed to be the embryo of the history presented in separate accounts of important events as it was said to be an account of important historical events according to certain classification. Thus, we could see the endeavors of historians for a new style of historiography, despite the fact that no one could delineate its true picture. In a sense, however, the loss of the book also suggests that it was not mature yet, which in turn means that it lacked necessary objective conditions at that time.

By Yuan Shu's time in the Southern Song Dynasty things had completely been different. Sima Guang's *History as a Mirror for Governance*, while pushing the annalistic style of history to its zenith, laid a solid foundation for the emergence of the new style of history presented in separate accounts of important events.

The main difference between the two styles of history lies in the fact that the former records history in terms of time, i.e. in chronological order, while the latter does it in terms of major historical events. In *History as a Mirror for Governance*, both methods were used in the organization of historical materials, although the former was the predominant one. This can be illustrated by many examples.

In the book, important events were recorded at one stretch as coherent and relatively independent stories. Such events might have lasted for several days, several months, several years, or even several decades. Under the entry of the first lunar month of the first year of Jiaping Period (249 A.D.) in the seventh volume, for example, the author gave a vivid description of the whole process of the five-day court coup d'état in which Sima Yi murdered Cao Shuang. Another example is the account of the Battle of Feishui under the entry of the eighth year of the Taiyuan

Period (383 A.D.) in the one hundred and fifth volume. It gives a clear account of how Fu Jian issued the order to recruit soldiers in the seventh year, how the expedition started in the eighth lunar month, how the army of the Eastern Jin Dynasty deployed its troops in the ninth month, how it conquered the cities of Shouyang and Yuncheng in the tenth month, how the first battle was fought at Luojian and great victory was gained at Feishui in the eleventh month, and how in the twelfth month Fu Jian returned to Chang'an, and General Xie Shi of the Jin Dynasty and others were rewarded for their military exploits, and all this is done in over 2,300 words. Still another example is the introduction of the book, which is about how King Weilie of the Zhou Dynasty granted fiefs to the three noble families of Wei, Zhao, and Han in the twenty-third year of his reign (403 B.C.). The author started from Zhi Xuanzi's proposal of appointing Zhi Yao as queen in the fourth year of the reign of King Yuan (470B.C.). The whole event covered nearly seven decades, and yet it was recorded succinctly. Later, the event of "Three Noble Families Dividing the State of Jin" in Yuan Shu's book was virtually a verbatim copy of this part.

In the recording of a particular historical period, *History as a Mirror for Governance* often gives prominence to major events by focusing on one or two of them while touching upon other minor ones. This is because important events normally lasted a relatively long time, during which some minor events that are worth recording might have happened. If these events were all recorded chronologically without a distinction between those significant and insignificant ones, there would be no focus in the book. In order to trace the rise and fall of the preceding dynasties clearly, Sima Guang adopted the method of focusing on major events. In treating the period from the sixth year of the Guanghe Period (183 A.D.) to the second lunar month of the second year of the Zhongping Period (185 A.D.), for example, he devoted most of the space to the Yellow Scarf Uprising (184–185 A.D.) besides brief mentioning of such events as the change of reign titles, major natural disasters and plagues, and the promotion of certain top officials, etc. Other minor peasant uprisings, such as those which broke out at Jiaozhi, Ba Prefecture and in the north, were mentioned in relation to the Yellow Scarf Uprising and served to give prominence to it. Another example is the description of the An Lushan Rebellion that lasted from the first lunar month of the twelfth year of the Tianbao Period (754) to the eighth lunar month of the first year of the Zhide Period (756). With several ten thousand words, the author gave a detailed account of the activities and attitudes of the emperor, high officials, generals, civilians, and the rebels, unfolding a vivid historical scroll of that turbulent event which was the turning point of the Tang Dynasty from prosperity to decline. Meanwhile, he mentioned a number of other events, which served to facilitate the readers' understanding of the social background of the rebellion. Thanks to this method of focusing on important events, the book was able to record complicated historical events without confusing readers. For while recording history in the chronological order with a focus on the central or major events of the periods concerned, this method enabled the author to prune away or merely touch upon minor events that were unrelated or barely related to the major events. The author's attention was thus on "the event" rather than "the time" when it took place. Thus, the book paved the way for the appearance of the event-focus style of history presented in separate accounts of important events.

As regards those minor events that were worth mentioning but not important enough to warrant independent entries, *History as a Mirror for Governance* often touched upon them while recounting a similar major event. This method was created by Xun Yue in *the Annals of the Han Dynasty*, but Sima Guang inherited and perfected it. One of the ways was to put similar events or historical figures together. During the Jin Dynasty, for instance, a famous scholar Ruan Ji was criticized for gambling, playing chess games and getting drunk while observing mourning for his mother; Ruan Xian was infamous for his affairs with his favorite maid servant; Liu Lin was known as a notorious drunkard; and Ji Kang ignored an important official visitor when he was working with iron. These four things did not take place in the same year, but Sima Guang still grouped them together under the entry of Ji Kang's death, as the four men were among the "seven famous scholars of bamboo groves" (i.e. they were known for their love of bamboo groves) who believed in nihilism and disdained laws and regulations. Another way was to contrast events of opposite nature. For instance, the mentioning of Ji Shao's acceptance of the appointment of vice director of the imperial secretariat in the tenth year of the Taishi Period (274 A.D.), twelve years after his father Ji Kang was wrongly killed by the emperor, was immediately followed by a description of how Wang Pou, after his father Wang Yi was wrongly killed by the emperor, refused to accept any official position and finally died in poverty. They were not concurrent events either. The purpose of putting them together was to make a contrast and express the author's commendation of one and condemnation of the other. Still another way might be called "chain description". Under the entry of the first lunar month of the third year of the Taikang Period (283 A.D.) when Emperor Wudi of the Jin Dynasty came to the throne, the author recorded Liu Yi's criticism of the emperor, which was followed by his deposition of Yang Xiu, who competed with Wang Kai and Shi Cong in showing off their affluence, which finally led to Fu Xian's memorial to the emperor in which he advocated encouragement of frugality and discouragement of extravagance, although those events did not all happen in the third year of the Taikang Period. In adopting this method of recording historical events, Sima Guang had in reality deviated from the "time focus" norm of the annalistic style and assimilated the "event focus" of the history presented in separate accounts of important events.

In *History as a Mirror for Governance*, Sima Guang used the flashback method in the recording of historical events by giving an account of their causes first before describing the events themselves. Following the style of *Zuo's Commentary*, he often used phrases like "at the very beginning" to indicate the distant causes of an event. In the description of the dispute between Yuandi of the Jin Dynasty and Wang Dun in the third year of the Taixing Period (320), for example, he started the passage with the sentence "at the very beginning when the emperor conquered the east of the Yangtze River". Obviously, this is at variance with the annalistic style because it contains some elements of the "event focus" style.

Furthermore, Sima Guang also supplemented the accounting of

historical events by mentioning their consequences. An example in point is the entry of the third year of the First Emperor of the Qin Dynasty (244 B.C.). Under this entry he described how Prince Zhao wisely appointed Li Mu general of his army in defense of his fief against the invasion of the Huns. At the end of the entry, he added, "The chieftain of the Huns fled in panic, and dared not even approach the border for over a while decade." The book also contains many sentences like "in the end, the whole thing did not come off" or "he finally failed". This style of describing events is already indistinguishable from that of the history presented in separate accounts of important events.

From the examples cited above in illustration of the methods adopted by Sima Guang, one can clearly perceive that, while following the tradition of the annalistic style, he often deviated from the conventional way of "putting the events strictly under relevant dates" and created the method of adhering to the time-focus principle while giving due consideration to the event-focus principle. This exhibited the tendency of his time to deviate from the annalistic style of historiography, which also paved the way for Yuan Shu to establish the style of history presented in separate accounts of important events.

Yuan Shu, whose courtesy name was Jizhong, was born in the Prefecture of Jian'an (today's Jian'ou County of Fujian Province) in the Southern Song Dynasty. A diligent scholar since his childhood, he became a *jinshi* during the Longxing Period of Emperor Xiaozong (1163–1164), whereupon he was appointed administrative assistant to the magistrate of the Prefecture of Wenzhou. In the seventh year of the Qiandao Period (1171), he was promoted lecturer in the court. As his proposals were not adopted by the emperor and he found it difficult to get along with some powerful officials, he submitted a request to be transferred to the Prefecture of Yanzhou as an instructor, which was promptly approved. He loved Sima Guang's book, but he found that the arrangement of a multitude of historical materials under entries of dates in the book often confused readers, since many events had spanned several years. Besides, as so many important events had taken place during the one thousand three hundred and sixty-two years covered by the book, readers often had to refer to many volumes in order to get a complete picture of an event, including its causes, process, and results. This inspired his idea of writing something to make up for this defect, which eventuated in the book *History as a Mirror for Governance Topically Arranged.*

Yuan Shu's book, as its title suggests, is a rearrangement of the materials in *History as a Mirror for Governance* according to their topics with the "event-focus" method. Each section of the book has an independent title and records a complete event. The whole book consists of forty-two volumes with two hundred and thirty-nine sections, arranged chronologically from the division of the State of Jin by the States of Han, Zhao, and Wei towards the end of the Spring and Autumn Period to the punitive expedition of Huainan by Emperor Shizong of the Latter Zhou Dynasty (951–960).

Yuan Shu completed the book in only two years during his term as an instructor in the Prefecture of Yanzhou. This shows that the time and energy he expended could not be mentioned at the same breath with those of Sima Guang. Besides, all the materials in his book were taken from Sima Guang's book. Later scholars, therefore, held that his book had neither any valuable historical materials nor any original views worthy of scholarly attention. Zhang Xuecheng of the Qing Dynasty, for example, said that Yuan Shu had no intention of creating a new style of historiography in the first place, that he was not even learned enough to accomplish such an important undertaking, and that the new style was just an accidental attainment. Liang Qichao of the Qing Dynasty expressed a similar opinion in his book *Research Methodology of Chinese History.* He remarked that Yuan's book only served to facilitate the reading of Sima Guang's great work, and that it was merely a partial copy of the latter in the form of a new book. In short, the creation of the new style of historiography was made without any conscious effort on the part of the author, and his book was no more than an appendage to that of Sima Guang.

Nevertheless, the significance of the history presented in a series of important events created by Yuan Shu for the renovation of Chinese historiography won the unanimous commendation of scholars, including even Zhang Xuecheng and Liang Qichao. When the book was first published, famous scholars of the Southern Song Dynasty Zhu Xi, Yang Wanli, and Lü Zuqian wrote prefaces and postscripts in which they lavished praises upon it. Zhu Xi, for example, wrote in the postscript: The fact that some of the events recorded in *History as a Mirror for Governance* lasted for decades or even centuries made it difficult for readers to keep track of them since there were no cohesion and coherence between the different parts of the book. Yuan Shu's book, on the other hand, presented the complete pictures of these events since they were all recorded in independent sections. Yang Wanli remarked in the preface that it was a "must for rulers" because it provided profound analyses for the causes of the fall of the past dynasties and offered remedies for them. He further observed that it was "a must for ordinary readers" as well who, instead of being baffled by the disjointed pieces of information about an event under separate entries of different years, were now enabled to "live" with the historical personages, sharing their weal and woe, and laughing and weeping for the vicissitudes of their lives. These comments were echoed by Lü Zuqian, who said that the book presented historical events as organic wholes, so that readers could easily understand Sima Guang's views. It was indeed a difficult undertaking that made the learning of history an easier job.

If the praises of Zhu Xi, Yang Wanli, and Lü Zuqian reflected their personal affections since they were close friends of Yuan Shu, the multitude of criticisms by scholars of the late Ming and early Qing Dynasties were more convincing. The preface to the new edition of *History as a Mirror for Governance Topically Arranged* published in the Ming Dynasty, for example, pointed out that, just as no one could learn the history of the preceding dynasties without reading *History as a Mirror for Governance*, no one could fully comprehend this book without referring to *History as a Mirror for Governance Topically Arranged*. In this sense, Yuan Shu's contribution could be equated with that of Sima Guang. Ji Yun, a well-known scholar in the Qing Dynasty, remarked in his *A Synoptic Catalogue of the Complete Library of Four Treasuries* that Yuan's book was an unprecedented monumental work that integrated two styles of historiography, i.e. the annalistic and chronological-biographical styles of historiography, which offered a clear picture of the historical events in the previous millennium. Another scholar Zhang Xuecheng commented that, thanks to its event-focus method, the book was much more succinct than chronological-biographical histories and much clearer than annals in the presentation of events, and he commended it as a masterpiece for its judgment of right and wrong and skillful selection of materials. Liang Qichao was even more generous in his praise. He said that the event-focus method was indispensable for the analysis of the causes and consequences of historical events both as a mirror for the past and as a lesson for the future, and he concluded that the history presented in separate accounts of important events was closest to the ideal style of historiography and the natural result of the evolution of older styles of historiography.

Needless to say, not all the comments cited above were impeccable, but one thing is clear, that is, the new style of history made up for the defects of the annalistic and chronological-biographical styles of history. With the birth of this new style of historiography marked by the publication of *History as a Mirror for Governance Topically Arranged*, Chinese historiography entered a new age with the three co-existing major styles — the time-focus style of the annals, the people-focus style of chronological-biographical history, and the event-focus style of history presented in separate accounts of important events.

Looking back at the relationship between this new style of history and *History as a Mirror for Governance*, one can easily perceive the profound influence of this magnum opus on it. In the first place, Yuan's book was a direct adaptation of Sima Guang's book. In the second place, Yuan got all the historical materials and views about historical events from Sima Guang's book, not to mention the fact that his motive for writing this book was inspired by the latter. In the third place, even the style of Yuan's book still had traces of the annals. It consisted of two hundred and thirty-nine sections arranged strictly in chronological order, and the events recorded in each section were also arranged in accordance with the requirements of the annalistic style. In this sense, the history presented in separate accounts of important events could be considered a new branch of the annalistic style of historiography. Furthermore, some of the breakthroughs made by *History as a Mirror for Governance* in the annalistic style of historiography discussed above also laid a foundation for the creation of this new style by Yuan. From all this we can safely conclude that there would be no *History as a Mirror for Governance Topically Arranged* without *History as a Mirror for Governance*, nor could this new style of historiography have emerged.

If *History as a Mirror for Governance* exerted a direct influence on the writing of *History as a Mirror for Governance Topically Arranged*, the latter rewarded it by promoting its popularization and reception.

The history presented in separate accounts of important events was marked by two dominant features. One was the simplification of complicated historical phenomena, which made it much easier for readers to remember them; the other was its story-telling method in describing the rise and fall of the preceding dynasties, which appealed to readers. These features made *History as a Mirror for Governance Topically Arranged* much more easily accessible to learners of history than Sima Guang's book. This is because the best way for readers to get a clear view of complicated things like history is to start from certain key points (i.e. events) to the lines, which delineate the whole picture. As various historical phenomena are interrelated to one another, it would be easier to study the beginning, development, and ending of events as well as their mutual relations by studying individual events first. The complicated processes of many historical events were not clearly presented in chronological-biographical histories and annals, but in *History as a Mirror for Governance Topically Arranged* they were accounted for one by one as complete stories, which helped readers grasp a general picture of history quickly. Therefore, it was not only a good introductory book to *History as a Mirror for Governance* for students of history, but also an effective promotor of its influence.

However, despite its merits of clear presentation and high comprehensibility, *History as a Mirror for Governance Topically Arranged* could not take the place of *History as a Mirror for Governance*. It was only half the length of the latter with most of the important materials in Sima Guang's book, but it missed many less important, and, in some sections, even some important materials. In other words, Yuan's book could not be mentioned in the same breath with Sima Guang's book in terms of the richness and extensiveness of historical materials in them. Except for the convenience of finding materials related to certain topics, one still had to rely on the latter for information. Thus, the former is merely a reference book for the latter. When it comes to the quoting of original materials, one still has to refer to the latter.

Incorporating the merits of the annalistic and chronological-biographical histories while avoiding their major shortcomings, the style of history with separate accounts of important events emerged as the third major style of Chinese historiography, and soon it underwent rapid development as numerous history books were written in imitation of Yuan Shu's book. This trend was initiated by two books, i.e. *Events in Spring and Autumn Annals and Zuo's Commentary Topically Arranged* by Zhang Chong and *History of the Imperial Song Dynasty As a Mirror for Governance Topically Arranged* by Yang Zhongliang. By the Ming and Qing Dynasties, there were already hundreds of history books written in the style established by Yuan Shu, thus forming an independent genre of historiography. Its importance was further enhanced by the authorized version of *A Synoptic Catalogue of the Complete Library of Four Treasuries* published in the reign of Emperor Qianlong of the Qing Dynasty in which there is an independent section for history in the event-focus style.

After the publication of Yuan Shu's book, the event-focus style of history branched off in two directions: One was about dynastic histories; and the other was about specific histories.

By the modern times, histories of all the dynasties had versions in the event-focus style which, if pieced together, would form a complete general history of China with separate accounts of important events. The most important of history books of this style include:

1. *Remote History as a Mirror for Governance Topically Arranged* by Shen Chaoyang in one hundred volumes, which was a history of the

time prior to what was recorded in Sima Guang's book presented in the event-focus style.

2. *Events in Zuo's Commentary Topically Arranged* by Gao Shiqi of the Qing Dynasty in fifty-three volumes, which presented history clearly under specific topics on the basis of Zhang Chong's *Events in Spring and Autumn Annals and Zuo's Commentary Topically Arranged*. It was placed on a par with Zhang Chong's book by *A Synoptic Catalogue of the Complete Library of Four Treasuries*.

3. *History of the Song Dynasty Topically Arranged* by Chen Bangzhan of the Ming Dynasty in twenty-six volumes, which was a sequel to Yuan Shu's book and an expanded version of the unpublished manuscript of Feng Qi of the Ming Dynasty. The book is mainly based on the historical events recorded in the official histories of the Song, Liao, Jin, and Yuan Dynasties, including abundant information about their political systems and cultural aspects. With its vivid descriptions and lucid presentation, it is considered a must for studies of the Song Dynasty.

4. *History of the Liao Dynasty Topically Arranged* by Li Youtang of the Qing Dynasty in forty volumes.

5. *History of the Jin Dynasty Topically Arranged* by Li Youtang of the Qing Dynasty in fifty-two volumes, which is mutually complementary with *History of the Liao Dynasty Topically Arranged*.

6. *History of the Western Xia Dynasty Topically Arranged* by Zhang Jian of the Ming Dynasty in thirty-six volumes.

7. *History of the Yuan Dynasty Topically Arranged* by Chen Bangzhan of the Ming Dynasty in four volumes, which is mainly based on the official *History of the Yuan Dynasty* and *Sequel to A General Outline of History as a Mirror for Governance*[1] but is not as substantial as *History of the Song Dynasty Topically Arranged* in content.

8. *History of the Ming Dynasty Topically Arranged* by Gu Yingtai of the

---

[1] *A General Outline of History as a Mirror for Governance*, compiled by Zhu Xi and finished by his disciple Zhao Shiyuan, offered a revision of *History as a Mirror for Governance* that was compatible with Zhu Xi's orthodox Confucian ideas.

Qing Dynasty in eighty volumes. Its authorship, however, is still disputable. Some people suspect that it might have been written by Tan Qian, or Xu Zhuodai, or Lu Qi, but most scholars today agree that its main author is Gu Yingtai. Another book, i.e. the six-volume *Supplement to History of the Ming Dynasty Topically Arranged*, which was published later, is also attributed to Gu Yingtai and others. In the Qing Dynasty, a scholar named Peng Sunyi wrote *Sequel to Events in the History of the Ming Dynasty* in five volumes, which supplied some of the historical events missing in Gu's books.

9. *History of the Three Feudatories Topically Arranged* by Yang Longrong of the Qing Dynasty in four volumes, which mainly recorded the history of the Southern Ming Dynasty.

10. *History of the Qing Dynasty Topically Arranged* by Huang Hongshou in eighty volumes, which recorded the history from the beginning of the Qing Dynasty to the reign of Emperor Guangxu (1875–1908), based mainly on *Records of the History of the East Flowery Empire*, as well as some stories circulated among the common people.

Despite the disparity in quality and academic value, those books, together with *History as a Mirror for Governance Topically Arranged*, present a complete general history of China from remote antiquity to the Qing Dynasty in the event-focus style, which marks the maturity of an independent system of historiography.

Apart from the dynastic histories of this style, there appeared many specific histories of the same style since the Ming and Qing Dynasties, which even outnumbered dynastic histories. The most well-known of them include: *the Records of the Southern Expedition* by Tian Rucheng of the Ming Dynasty about how Wang Shouren suppressed the rebellion of Cen Meng, *Records of the Suppression of Li Zicheng's Rebellion* by Wu Weiye of the Qing Dynasty, which starts from the breaking out of Li's uprising to the fall of the Ming Dynasty, *History of the Four Vassal States in the Early Qing Dynasty* by Qian Mingshi of the Qing Dynasty, which was about the lives of Wu

Sangui, Kong Youde, Geng Zhongming, and Shang Kexi, *a Short History of Taiwan* written at the imperial order of Emperor Qianlong, which is about the downfall of the Zhengs' rule in Taiwan, *the Suppression of the Rebellion in Jinchuan* by Lai Bao and others, and *the Suppression of the Rebellion in Junggar* by Fu Heng, etc. In modern times, such books included *the Suppression of the Rebellion in Guangdong Province* and *the Suppression of the Nian Army Rebellion* by Yixin and others, *Records of the Treaties between China and Other Countries* by Lu Yuanding, *the Sino-French War* and *the Sino-Japanese War* by Luo Chunrong, *History of the Westernization Movement* by Wen Qing, *Real History of the 1911 Revolution in Wuchang*, and *Sino-Japanese Relations in the Past Sixty Years*, etc.

Yuan Shu himself probably had never expected that his book would produce such an extensive and profound influence, but this influence, in the final analysis, should be attributed to Sima Guang for his *History as a Mirror for Governance*.

2. *History as a Mirror for Governance* and Histories in the Outline Style

The other type of adaptation of *History as a Mirror for Governance* was represented by *A General Outline of History as a Mirror for Governance*. Before we embark on a discussion of the book it is necessary to give a biographical sketch of its author Zhu Xi.

Zhu Xi, who had a courtesy name Yuanhui and an alternative name Hui'an, was born in Wuyuan County of Anhui Province. He passed the top-level imperial examination during the Shaoxing Period (1131–1162) of Emperor Gaozong in the Southern Song Dynasty and served four emperors, namely, Gaozong, Xiaozong, Guangzong, and Ningzong. Unsuccessful in his official career, he spent most of his life as a lecturer and writer. He is recognized as a master of Confucianism as his books incorporate all the essence of the principlistic philosophy of the Song Dynasty. His numerous books cover a wide range of branches of learning, including philosophy and literary criticism, as well as historiography. His historical works include *Records of the Words and Deeds of Famous Officials in the First Eight Reigns of the Song Dynasty* and *Origins of Neo-Confucian Philosophy*. The most influential one is *A General Outline of History as a Mirror for Governance*, of which he was the chief compiler. It was the first popular history book written in the outline style often used as a textbook aimed at maintaining the rule of feudal ethics.

Like Yuan Shu, Zhu Xi had a great esteem for Sima Guang. However, much as he loved *History as a Mirror for Governance*, he was not satisfied with it. He criticized it for confusing what was legitimate and what was illegitimate. In his view, it was unjustified to regard the Wei Dynasty as more legitimate than the Shu Han and Wu Dynasties and to use the names of the years named by later rulers instead of the original ones. Besides, he thought that Sima Guang's discussions about the relationship between one's learning and virtues was one-sided, and the parts of his book on the Tang Dynasty and the Five Dynasties seemed to be too prolix. In short, he held that the book was far from perfect as a mirror for governance, especially regarding the issue of "legitimism". A steadfast supporter of the Southern Song Dynasty which retained sovereignty over only a small part of the country then, he could not accept the idea of "regarding the Wei Dynasty as legitimate and the Shu Han Dynasty as illegitimate". Furthermore, he criticized the book for being far too detailed as a textbook of history for emperors. Therefore, he abridged and revised it into *A General Outline of History as a Mirror for Governance*.

The preface of the book was a rationale for the writing of the book, which boiled down to two points. One was its unnecessary lengthiness and prolixity, which drowned out the key points and made the reading a tough job. A more concise and comprehensible book was thus called for to overcome this shortcoming. The other point was its tendency to stray away from the track of legitimism, which necessitated the correction of its way of presentation. Zhu's ultimate purpose was to write a comprehensible and useful book as an aid for the governance of the ruling class, as well as for moral education. This point of departure determined the style and the selection of materials of the book.

Zhu Xi began to work at the book in about the third year of the Qiandao Period (1167). After laying down its stylistic rules and layout, he devoted all his energies to the writing work with the help of his student Zhao Shiyuan and his friends Cai Jitong, Li Bojian, Zhang Yuanshan, and Yang Boqi. At first, the work proceeded smoothly, but later, due to his failing health and eye disease, the progress slowed down. With the deterioration of his eye disease, the finalization of the manuscript practically came to a standstill. Consequently, the whole book remained half-finalized twenty years later. The finishing work was mainly done with the assistance of Zhao Shiyuan. Despite all this, however, the whole project was initiated and accomplished under the guidance of Zhu Xi, and both the style and contents of the book were determined by him.

A master of the principlism of the Song Dynasty, Zhu Xi attached great importance to the philosophy. He emphasized that "[O]one should read our ancient classics before reading any history". He even said that "[R]reading history is like watching people fighting with each other". All these showed that he regarded historiography as an instrument for the acquisition of knowledge and a way for the expounding of philosophical thoughts. In his view, what was important in history books was not so much historical facts as the way they were presented. He decided to adopt the presentation of *the Spring and Autumn Annals* by Kong zi, which put potential traitors and usurpers in constant fear. Thus the whole book was full of political preaching on dynastic legitimism and cardinal ethical guides and constant virtues.

The historical events recorded in *A General Outline of History as a Mirror for Governance* are roughly identical with those in *History as a Mirror for Governance*, which starts from the twenty-third year of the reign of King Weilie of the Zhou Dynasty (403 B.C.) and ends at the sixth year of the Xiande Period of Emperor Shizong of the Later Zhou Dynasty (959). These events, however, are described strictly in accordance with Zhu Xi's personal view of legitimism, and those events which are presented differently in *History as a Mirror for Governance* are all rewritten. With a keen interest in the subjective notion of legitimism, he put forward his own theory of legitimate rule: "He who governs a united country without being challenged by the princes and who keeps control of the whole judicial system is a legitimate ruler." Following this theory, he regarded the Zhou, Qin, Han, Jin, Sui, and Tang Dynasties as legitimate dynasties. He further classified two categories of legitimate dynasties. Those which established legitimate dynasties from nothing were called "initiated legitimate dynasties", such as the Qin, Western Jin, Sui, and Song Dynasties; and those which lost their rule of the country in the end were called "remaining legitimate dynasties", such as the Shu Han and Eastern Jin Dynasties. He was thus very critical of *History as a Mirror for Governance* for recording the Wei Dynasty as a legitimate dynasty and insisted that the Shu Han Dynasty should be given a legitimate status. In his book, all the legitimate and illegitimate naming of years and periods, enthroning of emperors, changes of reign titles, appointments of heirs to the throne, important imperial meetings, and conferrals of official titles were all strictly presented in separate sections. In other words, Zhu Xi's notion of legitimism runs through the whole book.

Abiding by the Confucian principles of "loyalty, filial piety, chastity and righteousness", Zhu Xi deleted or corrected all the records that he considered at variance with his notions of cardinal guides and constant virtues in *History as a Mirror for Governance*. For example, in the fifth lunar month of the third year of the Zhangwu Period (223A.D.) of Emperor Zhaolie of the Shu Han Dynasty, the Last Emperor succeeded to the throne and thereupon the reign title was changed into the Jianxin Period. The part of the year before that, in his opinion, should still be named Zhangwu in honour of the dead emperor, but in *History as a Mirror for Governance*, the first year of the Jianxin Period started from the first month of that calendar year, according to the principle laid down by Sima Guang. Zhu Xi expressed his strong criticism of this: It was not only at variance with the fact, but it betrayed the principle of "letting the king be a king, a minister a minister, the father a father, and the son a son". In his book, all such cases were corrected. Besides, he added many special comments in praise of those chaste women who had committed suicide for their dead husbands, which sufficiently revealed his intention of maintaining the feudal code of ethics with the help of the book.

From the above discussion, we can see that *A General Outline of History as a Mirror for Governance*, in the way historical facts are presented with a special emphasis on legitimacy, is a textbook of history that served the purpose of maintaining the feudal rule better than Sima Guang's book did. He Shan of the Yuan Dynasty pointed out the nature of the book in his discussion of "its emphasis on the notion of legitimacy and Confucian code of ethics as admonitions for readers".

Another purpose of Zhu Xi in writing this book was to supply a more concise and comprehensible version of *History as a Mirror for Governance*. As was mentioned above, Sima Guang had already made great efforts in reducing thirty million words of raw historical records to over three million words. For most readers, however, it was still too voluminous and difficult for the retrieval of information. In an attempt to solve this problem, Yuan Shu rewrote it in separate accounts of important events. The book was thus much shorter with much clearer presentation of information. Nevertheless, while his *History as a Mirror for Governance Topically Arranged* had the virtue of presenting historical events in their entirety, it suffered a number of demerits, such as the isolation of related events and lacking of systematicness, as well as inappropriate omission of many important facts. That was the reason why Zhu Xi created the outline-focus style of history — to present the historical facts in *History as a Mirror for Governance* in another way.

The general outline-focus style of historiography, according to Wang Yinglin, a renowned scholar of the Southern Song Dynasty, was an attempt to imitate the outline of *the Spring and Autumn Annals* and *Zuo's Commentary* in the collection of the best comments of Confucian scholars. In this book, the naming of the years strictly follows the legitimate dynastic reign titles. The general outline is printed in big characters while separate commentaries give detailed descriptions. The outline and details suggest that once the outline is grasped, the whole picture of history can be easily captured. The outline in fact is an imitation of Kong zi' presentation of the *Spring and Autumn Annals* to provide the gist of historical events in chronological order printed in big characters, which not only functioned as terse titles, but also indicated the authors' attitude. The author's notes, which are like the annotations of *Zuo's Commentary* on *the Spring and Autumn Annals*, are detailed accounts of events printed in small characters. The most important feature of *A General Outline of History as a Mirror for Governance*, therefore, is its conciseness — its length being only one-fifth of that of Sima Guang's book, as well as its enhanced clarity and comprehensibility.

With the above-mentioned feature, *A General Outline of History as a Mirror for Governance* obviously suits the average readers. Zhang Taiyan, a modern scholar, once said that it would take at least more than five years for ordinary readers to finish the whole set of *History as a Mirror for Governance*. Zhu Xi also remarked that it was too difficult for people of average memory. *A General Outline of History as a Mirror for Governance*, on the other hand, was much easier. A scholar named Zhu Guozhen in the Ming Dynasty, for example, finished it in three months, and he managed to commit all the facts to memory. Its influence was thus remarkably greater than that of *History as a Mirror for Governance*.

Needless to say, the appearance of Zhu Xi's book was not accidental. Judging from the development of the historical trend, it actually reflected the increasing demand of readers for more succinct and comprehensible history books, which became very pressing in the Southern Song Dynasty. It was in response to this call of history that Yuan Shu wrote *History as a Mirror for Governance Topically Arranged*. The same was true of Zhu Xi's case. Although his main purpose was to preach and maintain the principle of feudal ethics, the publication of the book itself added a new branch to the annalistic style, which was a new contribution to Chinese historiography.

Since its publication, *A General Outline of History as a Mirror for Governance* has received very different scholarly judgments, from increasingly positive from the Song Dynasty to the Yuan and Ming Dynasties, to increasingly negative since the later Ming Dynasty.

The book received scholarly criticisms as soon as it was completed in the Southern Song Dynasty. The historian Li Xinchuan, for instance, pointed out when it was still circulating in the form of a manuscript that it committed many undue omissions of historical events and occasional errors in the naming of the years though its outline was perfect. He ascribed such errors to Zhu Xi's assistants' lack of expertise in historiography. When Zhu Xi was still alive, Zhang Nanxuan wrote him a letter to the effect that his book should not follow Sima Guang's book too closely since it might have errors itself.

The first scholar to express high appreciation for *A General Outline of History as a Mirror for Governance* was Zhu Xi's follower Li Fangzi. Ten years after Zhu's death, i.e. the third year of the Jiading Period (1210), he got the manuscript of the book from Zhu's son Zhu Zai. He immediately decided to have it proofread and printed, and the book was finally issued in the whole country in the twelfth year of the Jiading Period. In the epilogue, he wrote, "The book presents the history of our country in strict accordance with the criteria of legitimism, and expounds profound historical lessons in succinct language. It has corrected numerous mistakes in the official histories of the preceding dynasties along the lines of the neo-Confucian philosophy. By rejuvenating the classic studies of historiography, it sets an extraordinary model for future generations of scholars". In his view, the book was without parallel since the appearance of *the Spring and Autumn Annals*.

Four decades later, another follower of Zhu Xi named Wang Bai expressed his ardent admiration for his mentor in the epilogue of his *Guide to the Use of An Outline of History as a Mirror for Governance* published in the first year of the Xianchun Period (1265). For him it had surpassed all other books of its kind in its creation of a new style of history since the publication of Sima Qian's *Records of the Historian*, and the thought running through the whole book could serve as absolute spiritual guidance for ages to come.

It is not difficult to see that *A General Outline of History as a Mirror for Governance* enjoyed a lofty status in the Southern Dynasty. Those who first pushed it to this position were Zhu Xi's followers. Their compliments, besides those for the new style of historiography, were predominantly on its philosophical thought. After they had set the tone, scholars of later generations gradually pushed it to a crescendo.

In the Yuan and Ming Dynasties, the study of *History as a Mirror for Governance* itself was not as popular as in the Southern Song Dynasty, but in the meantime *A General Outline of History as a Mirror for Governance* received increasing scholarly attention. The waxing and waning influences of the two books were due to many reasons. First, after the Yuan Dynasty, the study of Zhu Xi's thought became a popular undertaking, and naturally his book benefited from his aura. Second, it enjoyed more royal support since, with a greater emphasis on the maintaining of the code of feudal ethics, it was more useful for the consolidation of their rule. Third, just as the renowned contemporary bibliographer Wang Zhongmin pointed out, it was best received since it was neither too complicated like the original work of Sima Guang nor too simple like those abridged versions. Besides, it met the needs of those scholars who wanted to take imperial examinations. That accounts for the reason why it kept being reprinted until the middle of the fifteenth century. Last but not least, thanks to its succinctness, comprehensibility, and clear emphasis on key points, it was better received by average readers. It was thus only too natural that the "outline craze" lasted for such a long time after the Yuan Dynasty.

The "outline craze" mainly had two forms. One was the passion for annotations, interpretations, and verifications and error-corrections of the book; and the other was for the writing of sequels, supplements, and adaptations.

The book received the immediate attention of many scholars after its publication, most of whom made annotations, interpretations, and corrections for it. The first scholars to do verifications and corrections about the book were Li Xinchuan and Zhou Mi of the Southern Song Dynasty. Nevertheless, instead of writing monographs, they only included their discussions on it and corrections in their books titled *Miscellaneous Notes on the Events in the Court and among the Populace Since the Jianyan Period of the Southern Song Dynasty* and *Rustic Words of a Man from the Eastern Qi* respectively.

Things changed after the Song Dynasty, when there appeared a large variety of books about *A General Outline of History as a Mirror for Governance*. In the Yuan Dynasty, there were the *Exposition of a General Outline of History as a Mirror for Governance* by Yin Qixin, *the Presentation of Events in A General Outline of History as a Mirror for Governance* by Liu Youyi, *A Study of Different Versions of the Guides in A General Outline of History as a Mirror for Governance* by Wang Kekuan, *Collected Readings of A General Outline of History as a Mirror for Governance* by Wang Youxue, *A Textual Research on A General Outline of History as a Mirror for Governance* by Xu Zhaowen, and *A Tentative Study of A General Outline of History as a Mirror for Governance* by He Zhong. In the Ming Dynasty, the "outline craze" remained unabated. The most well-known books on Zhu Xi's book included *the Subtle Meanings of A General Outline of History as a Mirror for Governance* by Wang Feng, *Research on the Real Meanings of A General Outline of History as a Mirror for Governance* by Feng Zhishu, and *A Sequel to A General Outline of History as a Mirror for Governance* by Zhang Zixun. In the Qing Dynasty, scholars continued to publish their monographs on it, which included *Supplementary Annotations of A General Outline of History as a Mirror for Governance* by Rui Changxu, *Errors in A General Outline of History as a Mirror for Governance* by Chen Jingyun, *Corrections of A General Outline of History as a Mirror for Governance* by Feng Ban, *the Underlying Meanings and Corrections of A General Outline of History as a Mirror for Governance* and *the Underlying Meanings and Supplementary Notes on A General Outline of History as a Mirror for Governance* by Zhang Geng, *Queries on A General Outline of History as a Mirror for Governance* by Hua Zhan'en, and *Random Notes on A General Outline of History as a Mirror for Governance* by Zou Shurong, etc.

The number and scope of the books on the theory, thought, and presentation of Zhu Xi's book and those which annotated it and corrected its errors far exceeded those on Sima Guang's book. The influence of Zhu's book, if we take into account *the Authorized Version of A General Outline of History as a Mirror for Governance*, *the Authorized Version of Selected Readings from A General Outline of History as a Mirror for Governance*, and *the*

Third Edition of A General Outline History as a Mirror for Governance published with the approval of Emperors Kangxi and Qianlong of the Qing Dynasty, seemed even greater than that of Sima Guang's book.

Interestingly, while pointing out the errors and mistakes in *A General Outline of History as a Mirror for Governance*, many scholars, such as Wang Kekuan, Zhang Zixun, Rui Changxu, and Chen Jingyun, all refrained from criticizing Zhu Xi himself. Instead, they attributed all the errors and mistakes either to his students, or to the scholars who copied it, or to the printing houses. Even those most critical scholars, such as Quan Zuwang and Zhang Taiyan, asserted that it was not a worthy book mainly because they did not think it was written by Zhu Xi himself. This fact itself was an indication of the tremendous influence of Zhu Xi in the later stage of feudal China.

Just as Yuan Shu's *History as a Mirror for Governance Topically Arranged* was imitated by many scholars, Zhu Xi's book was followed by numerous sequels, supplementary and adapted works, and thus there formed a series of general histories along the lines of the outline-focus style.

The first sequel to Zhu Xi's book was the eighteen-volume *Pre-sequel to A General Outline of History as a Mirror for Governance* by Jin Lüxiang of the Southern Song Dynasty. Like the pre-sequels to *History as a Mirror for Governance*, Jin's book records the history before the twenty-third year of the reign of King Weilie of the Zhou Dynasty in the outline-focus style, the only difference being that it starts from the time of Emperor Yao (2447–2307 B.C.). At the turn of the Yuan and Ming Dynasties, a scholar called Chen Jing wrote a twenty-four-volume *Sequel to History as a Mirror for Governance*, which, despite its title, was more like a *Sequel to A General Outline of History as a Mirror for Governance* as most of its annotations were written in the outline-focus style. The first volume of the book starts from the time of Pan Gu, the creator of the universe in Chinese mythology and ends in the Period of Di Ku (2480–2345 B.C.). The second volume is sort of supplement, which is about the history of Qidan ethnic group during the Tang Dynasty and the Five Dynasties. The other twenty-two volumes are a post sequel to Zhu Xi's book, which records the history of the Song

Dynasty from Emperor Taizu till the end of the Southern Song Dynasty.

In the early Ming Dynasty, a scholar named Hu Cuizhong published a sixteen-volume *Sequel to the History of the Yuan Dynasty*, which starts from the thirteenth year of the Zhiyuan Period of Emperor Shizu (1276) and ends in the twenty-eighth year of the Zhizheng Period of Emperor Shundi (1368). It is a kind of sequel to Chen Jing's book in the outline-focus style in imitation of *A General Outline of History as a Mirror for Governance*.

Following Chen's and Hu's books, Chen Renxi, Xü (许) Hao, Nan Xuan, and Xü (徐) Hao of the Ming Dynasty wrote four books of the same name *Pre-sequel to A General Outline of History as a Mirror for Governance* with basically the same contents. This fact itself is also sufficient evidence of the popularity of Zhu Xi's book.

Another book that is worth mentioning is the twenty-seven-volume *Sequel to A General Outline of History as a Mirror for Governance* by Shang Lu and others, which was written under the imperial order during the Chenghua Period (1465–1487) of the Ming Dynasty. It is an official record of the history of the Song and Yuan Dynasties with Chen Jing's and Hu Cuizhong's books as the original versions. Just as Zhu Xi selected his materials from *History as a Mirror for Governance*, Shang Lu and his co-authors should also have had a good version of *Sequel to History as a Mirror for Governance* from which they could select source materials. Unfortunately, at that time Xue Yingqi and Wang Zongmu's *History of the Song and Yuan Dynasties as a Mirror for Governance* had not been published yet, not to mention the *Sequel to History of the Song and Yuan Dynasties as a Mirror for Governance* by Xu Qianxue and Bi Yuan. It is thus only too natural that Shang Lu's book has some undesirable lapses and omissions.

For reasons mentioned above, Emperor Kangxi of the Qing Dynasty ordered that Zhu Xi's book and its pre-sequel be combined into an authorized version. Later, in the reigns of Emperors Kangxi and Yongzheng a scholar named Zhang Tingyu wrote *A General Outline of History as a Mirror for Governance in the Third Part* in forty volumes under the imperial order, which aimed at continuing Zhu Xi's book as the main part, Shang Lu and others' *Sequel to A General Outline of History as a Mirror for Governance* as the second part, and the history of the Ming Dynasty which they added as the third part. As Emperor Qianlong was not satisfied with it, a revised version was published in the fortieth year of the Qianlong Period (1775) entitled *the Authorized Version of A General Outline of History as a Mirror for Governance in the Third Part.*

However, the outline-focus style of historiography did not continue to enjoy much popularity in the modern times as did the even-focus style. After the publication of *A General Outline of History as a Mirror for Governance in the Third Part*, the craze for it soon cooled down. The waning of its influence was probably due to the mounting criticisms against it since the late Ming and early Qing Dynasties.

The first important scholar to challenge the practice of "favoring *A General Outline of History as a Mirror for Governance* over *History as a Mirror for Governance* itself" was Gu Yanwu, a well-known thinker of the late Ming and early Qing Dynasties. Having studied Sima Guang's book since he was eleven years old, Gu deplored the fact that "Most people read only '*A General Outline*'". He was strongly against adapting the works of previous scholars, especially taking them as their own works. In his eyes, Zhu Xi's book, being an adaptation, could not possibly be better than the original book itself. This was the first time *A General Outline of History as a Mirror for Governance* had been ranked inferior to Sima Guang's book.

During the reign of Emperor Qianlong, a prominent historian Quan Zuwang expressed veiled criticisms against Emperors Kangxi and Qianlong for "authorizing" *A General Outline of History as a Mirror for Governance* and including it in the *Complete Library of Four Treasuries*. He not only criticized Zhu Xi's book as a pile of worthless paper, but also scathingly satirized those who had praised it as "the number one book since the publication of *the Spring and Autumn Annals*" as "sycophants".

The modern scholar Zhang Taiyan pointed out that even Zhu Xi himself did not take his own book very seriously, and therefore, those who had attempted to enshrine it were at most village teachers. He firmly held that the only unchangeable model for writers of annals was *History as a Mirror for Governance.*

After that, Zhu Xi's book suffered increasing depreciation. By the 1911 Revolution, the outline-focus style itself had become obsolete.

The vicissitudes of *A General Outline of History as a Mirror for Governance* coincided with the changes of the social status of Zhu Xi himself and his principlism. When his philosophy enjoyed the dominant official status, his book, which represented this philosophy, was naturally revered as orthodox philosophy and enjoyed a high status. From the late Ming and early Qing Dynasties onward, when his philosophy met with increasing challenges and his own influence was on the wane, the book was taken out of the shrine. The academic value of *A General Outline of History as a Mirror for Governance* was undeniably much lower than that of *History as a Mirror for Governance*. The fact that the former had been favored over the latter was simply due to political factors. Therefore, it was only too natural to lower the status of the former to what it deserves, although politics also played an important part there. Meanwhile, the creation of the outline-focus style, as well as its status and influence in the history of popular literature, should be given due appraisal.

As regards the relationship between *History as a Mirror for Governance* and the outline-focus style of history, one should also mention another craze for the annals, i.e. the "outline-mirror craze" which prevailed for a short period.

The outline-mirror style of history was in vogue at the same time as the outline-focus style of history, and was closely related to it. Chai Degeng (1908–1970) observed that the former was in fact a simplified form of the latter. In other words, the former contained much fewer historical events and was written much more succinctly than the latter. It was a kind of simplified annals for the common people written according to the principle of "rather be simple than complicated, and rather be popular than elevated".

The first book of the outline-mirror style was *The Outline-Mirror of the Dynasties* by Zhao Shiji of the mid-Ming Dynasty, which received immediate welcome upon its publication for its succinctness and simplicity, and was for a time even more popular than *A General Outline of History as a Mirror for Governance*. At that time it was a fashion for those ostentatious men of letters and high-ranking officials to show off their knowledge by forging histories in the outline-mirror style, the most well-known of which included *The Outline-Mirror of Historical Events* by Wang Shizhen, *A Gist of the Outline-Mirror of History*, *A Short Outline-Mirror of Official History* by Gu Xichou, *Dafang Outine-Mirror of History* by Li Tingji, *Yutang Outline-Mirror of History* by Ye Xianggao, *Yuan Liaofan's Supplement to the Outline-Mirror of History* by Yuan Liaofan, etc. Even in the early Qing Dynasty, we had *A Brief Outline-Mirror of History* by Zhu Lin and *A Simplified Outline-Mirror of History* by Wu Chenquan.

Of all the books mentioned above, the most popular one was perhaps *A Simplified Outline-Mirror of History*. Its writer Wu Chenquan, who was one of the co-editors of *An Anthology of the Finest Ancient Prose*, was keenly aware of the needs of the common people. With the assistance of his friends Zhou Zhijiong and Zhou Zhican, he wrote the one-hundred-and-seven volume book with materials from Liu Shu's *Supplement to History as a Mirror for Governance*, Jin Lüxiang's *Pre-sequel to History as a Mirror for Governance*, Zhu Xi's *A General Outline of History as a Mirror for Governance*, Shang Lu's *Sequel to A General Outline of History as a Mirror for Governance*, and Gu Yingtai's *History of the Ming Dynasty Topically Arranged*, etc. An extremely simple general history from the Period of Pangu to the end of the Ming Dynasty in the outline-focus style, it is considered a representative work of the outline-mirror style of history. Soon after its publication, the outline-mirror craze cooled down. However, like *An Anthology of the Finest Ancient Prose*, this book was widely spread as a guide book for learners of the history of ancient China.

Despite their minor stylistic differences, Sima Guang's *History as a Mirror for Governance*, Zhu Xi's *A General Outline of History as a Mirror for Governance*, and Wu Chenquan's *A Simplified Outline-Mirror of History* are all annals. The only difference is that Sima Guang's book is like a towering tree, while the other two are its branches.

Chapter Five

The Social Influence of
History as a Mirror for Governance

In the above chapters, we have discussed the major contributions of the monumental ancient history book *History as a Mirror for Governance* and its influence on the development of historiography after the Song Dynasty. The influence of the book on later generations, however, is not limited to that. As a matter of fact, in the nine centuries since its publication, people of all social classes in China, from emperors to officials and common people, have read it out of different attitudes and from different perspectives, and have drawn different historical lessons. Indeed, this great encyclopedic work has penetrated its extensive and profound influence into all aspects of the political and cultural life of Chinese society. In what follows, we will have a brief discussion of the relationships between this book and various sectors of Chinese society in illustration of its profound influence.

1. Emperors of the Feudal Dynasties and *History as a Mirror for Governance*

Liang Qichao once said that before he wrote a book, he would define its putative readership first, in order for it to produce the desired effect like a river that ran its course within its banks. He also said that *History as a Mirror for Governance* was meant for emperors and, therefore, it contained all necessary knowledge for them and omitted all things that were irrelevant to this purpose. Thus it was an ideal "textbook for emperors". This comment reveals the main purpose of Sima Guang in writing this book.

This purpose was also confirmed by Sima Guang's own words. In his *Memorial for Presenting History as a Mirror for Governance*, he clearly expressed his wish that Emperor Shenzong could "read it from time to time, use the rise and fall of the preceding dynasties as a mirror to reflect on the gains and losses of today, encourage what is good and discourage what is evil, adopt the correct ways and shy away from the wrong ones." In other words, he wished to provide historical lessons for emperors like Emperor Shenzong by his accounts of specially selected events. This determined the predominantly political nature of the contents in the book, which concentrated on the rise and fall of the preceding dynasties, the good and bad politics, and wise and fatuous emperors, as well as honest and dishonest officials.

Sima Guang attached great importance to the ways of emperors, because he held that "the governance of the country depends entirely on the emperors". Based on their competence and achievements, he classified the monarchs in Chinese history into five categories, i.e. those who established new dynasties, those who managed to keep their dynasties in good shape, those who stopped their dynasties from declining, those who brought declining dynasties back to prosperity, and those who lost the reign of the country. The first category of monarchs referred to those "exceedingly wise and brave emperors", such as Emperor Gaozu of the Han Dynasty who united the whole country, Emperor Wendi of the Sui Dynasty who was noted for his political reform, and Emperor Taizong of the Tang Dynasty under whose reign the country enjoyed great prosperity. Their achievements were recorded in detail and in copiously eulogistic language. The second category of monarchs "worked hard in accordance with the laws and moral standards laid down by their predecessors. They made every endeavor to close any loopholes in them and prevent them from becoming obsolete, so that the elderly people would not sigh over the passage of golden old days". The representatives of such emperors included Emperors Wendi and Jingdi of the Han Dynasty, and Emperor Xiaowendi of the Wei Dynasty. The fourth category of monarchs were "those talented emperors who disciplined themselves", respected virtuous people, and were always ready to learn whatever was good and correct whatever was wrong, so that they were able to "battle and beat social turbulence, bring peace and prosperity back to troubled and declining dynasties". Sima Guang ranked Emperor Xuandi of the Han Dynasty the top one of such emperors and poured on him profuse eulogies. These three types of emperors were undoubtedly the models from whom Sima Guang wished later emperors would learn.

On the other hand, Sima Guang vehemently attacked the third type of monarchs who failed to stop their dynasties from declining, such as Emperors Yuandi and Chengdi of the Western Han Dynasty, and Emperors Huandi and Lingdi of the Eastern Han Dynasty, who were "never bored with sumptuous meals and indolence, unable tell the loyal from the treacherous, blind to the gains and losses of things, and were content with temporary peace without any foresight of possible dangers", and the fifth type of monarchs were those who lost the reign of the country, such as the Last Emperor of the Chen Dynasty, and Emperor Yangdi of the Sui Dynasty, who "abandoned virtues for evils, and moral etiquette for carnal pleasure, who put sycophant officials in important positions and slaughtered honest officials despite the fury of heaven and the discontent of the common people".

When classifying emperors into five categories, Sima Guang emphasized that they were not unchangeable. The first, second and fourth types of monarchs could become the third and fifth types, and vice versa. The key to such transformations lay in whether they would take counsel with their subjects, and whether they would correct their errors or gloss over them, and how they chose the right people for official positions.

It was apparent that Sima Guang intended to use the deeds of different categories of monarchs as a mirror, hoping that emperors of later generations would learn from good examples and draw lessons from those bad ones. He repeatedly elaborated on "the ways of good emperors" and the possibilities of transformation between different types of emperors with a view to keeping later emperors on the alert for dangers of bad transformation all the time, and "carrying forward all the ancient virtues and achieving unprecedented peace and prosperity".

Sima Guang did not do all this in vain. Indeed, starting from Emperor Shenzong of the Song Dynasty, a good number of the emperors, who were the most important part of its readership, exhibited great enthusiasm for the book.

The greatest appreciation for the book, needless to say, came from Emperor Shenzong, who gave Sima Guang full support from the very beginning. Two months after he was enthroned in the first lunar month of the fourth year of the Zhiping Period (1067), the emperor promoted Sima Guang Hanlin Academician. In the tenth lunar month of the same year, he changed the original title of the book *Records of the Deeds of Emperors and Major Officials of the Past Ages* into *History as a Mirror for Governance*. He even wrote a preface for it himself and bestowed it on Sima Guang at a court meeting. Later, he bestowed on Sima Guang most of the books in the study of his former residence when he was Prince Ying. After Sima Guang came to Luoyang, he ordered him to submit the manuscript of each volume as soon as it was finished, which he would order other officials to read to him. Occasionally, he even requested new volumes before he finished reading the submitted ones. It should be pointed out that the emperor was extremely busy then as it was in the period of reform conducted by Prime Minister Wang Anshi. His keen interest in the book was sufficient indication of his seriousness about what he said in the preface, "We should explore the gains and losses of the preceding dynasties in order to carry forward the ways of benevolent governance and leave both good models and bad lessons to later generations." Obviously, this was more than mere insincere royal formality.

Before he left the capital in the first year of the Xining Period (1068), Sima Guang often read the finished parts of the book to Emperor Shenzong, who always listened with great interest. Once, in reply to the emperor's questions regarding the part about how Su Qin, an important politician in the Period of Warring States, served as prime minister of the six states at the same time, Sima Guang expounded his view, "Such political strategies as the alliance of states are no good for the governance of the country. I have included it in the book just to show the common practice of the time then. It is just for the reference of Your Majesty, so that Your Majesty might benefit from it by being on guard against it." At this the emperor said with admiration, "I can never get tired of listening to your reading of the book." Sima Guang often took the opportunity of reading the book to the emperor to express his political views, while the emperor was always ready to draw lessons from historical events. This example showed the great attraction of the book for emperors.

After the book was completed, Emperor Shenzong praised it as "an unprecedented book that is far superior to Xun Yue's *Annals of the Han Dynasty*" and promoted Sima Guang Academician of the Hall for Aid in Governance, which was another demonstration of the emperor's love for the book.

Another emperor who held Sima Guang and his book in high regard was Zhao Gou, Emperor Gaozong of the Southern Song Dynasty. According to historical records, Zhao Gou was a diligent scholar with outstanding intelligence and extensive knowledge. He has been despised by later generations for his trust of treacherous officials like Wang Boyan, Huang Qianshan and Qin Hui, and his failure to show any courage in face of foreign invasion, but, on the other hand, he was known as an expert in the study of *History as a Mirror for Governance*. Once he said to the imperial lecturer, "Sima Guang should really be respected for his courage to remonstrate with emperors." During his reign, the emperor issued a number of royal orders to reestablish the Department of Worthy and Excellent, Upright and Straight Remonstration which permitted the common people and even foreigners to discuss state affairs and put forward their suggestions. Despite its actual effect, his intention of drawing lessons from the historical records in the book allowed no doubt. Furthermore, in the fourth year of the Shaoxing Period (1134), he ordered his special envoy Zhang Yi to give a set of the book to the emperor of the Jin Dynasty as a present. This was further evidence of the lofty status of the book in his mind.

What was of great interest was the fact that both sides of the war then, i.e. Song and Jin, attached great importance to the study of *History as a Mirror for Governance*. As soon as he received the present of Emperor Gaozong, Emperor Taizong of the Jin Dynasty added it to the reading list of his crown prince. Obviously, this monarch of the Nuchen ethnic group had no less esteem for the book than the Han emperor did.

Similarly, Emperor Xiaozong of the Southern Song Dynasty also recommended this book to his crown prince. In *Selected Essays of Old Shuzhai on Study* by Sheng Ruzi, there is a dialogue between Emperor Xiaozong and his crown prince. One day the Emperor said to his son, "What are you reading these days besides *History as a Mirror for Governance*, which you are already very familiar with?" The crown prince replied, "Both Confucian classics and history books." And the Emperor urged him, "You should not neglect history while focusing on classics."

The above two examples are a vivid reflection of the fact that *History as a Mirror for Governance* was used as "a textbook for emperors". The crown princes of both the Song and Jin Dynasties were going to be emperors. Acquainting themselves with the book before acceding to the throne seemed to have become an essential step of preparation.

In the Qing Dynasty, Emperors Kangxi and Qianlong also showed great enthusiasm for the book, which was sufficiently demonstrated in the supreme authority of two books published by them, i.e. *Authorized Version of A General Outline of History as a Mirror for Governance* and *the Authorized Version of Selected Readings from A General Outline of History as a Mirror for Governance*. It should be pointed out, however, in an age of absolute monarchy, their recommendation of the book was only part of their endeavor to unify public thinking and consolidate their imperial power. Sima Guang himself said that education was the most important task of the government, and that social customs were a matter of paramount importance. He further remarked that only wise people would do their best to promote education and benefit from it. According to him, everyone, be he an emperor or a lowly civilian, should receive proper education and only through education could good unified social customs be cultivated. Therefore, *History as a Mirror for Governance* was, in a sense, an ideal textbook for this educational purpose. What interested the emperors of the dynasties was not so much how to be good emperors as how they should control their subjects and how officials should serve them. In fact, an important part of the book was on the ways of good officials.

2. Ancient Chinese Literati and *History as a Mirror for Governance*

In a long time after its publication, the main part of the readership of *History as a Mirror for Governance* was the literati. The reason was very simple. Sima Guang's first target group of readers were emperors, but most of them, not to mention those who failed to stop their dynasties from declining and those who lost the reign of the country, would not deign to read it themselves since they were accustomed to comfortable life. They would at most have their officials read it to them. As for the great masses of the common people, who had to work hard to make a precarious living and who had not received enough education to understand it, they could not possibly become a major part of its readership. Thus, in over one thousand years since its publication, the most profoundly influenced part of its readership was the literati.

Zhang Xuhou, a modern scholar, pointed out in his *History-Mirrorology* that Sima Guang wrote the book not only for emperors, but also for the literati, for while emperors needed to seek ways of prolonging their reigns, the literati should find ways of keeping their families from declining from historical lessons.

According to historical records, Sima Guang was known for his loyalty to his friends, and his modesty and honesty, as well as his courtesy. He said that he was just an ordinary man, but he had nothing on his conscience. He held "honesty" as his philosophy of life, whether he was "in a high official position" or "lived like a hermit". He was therefore considered a paragon of virtues for the literati in feudal China, especially in self-discipline.

Being such an honest man himself, Sima Guang expounds on the ways of good officials through the words of ancient saints in *History as a Mirror for Governance* as doctrines for later generations to abide by. From his authorial comments in the book, one could see that he attaches special importance to the ways of good subjects, the responsibilities of emperors and high officials, and self-discipline. He draws a clear line between the notions of proper rewards and punishments, benevolence and tyranny, righteousness and selfishness, faithfulness and deception, name and reality, ability and moral integrity, extravagance and frugality. Therefore, many people held that Sima Guang's book could not only serve as a textbook for emperors, but the ordinary literati could also learn much about ways of self-discipline and self-protection.

Along the lines of *the Spring and Autumn Annals*, Sima Guang's book lays an emphasis on the punishment of wickedness and encouragement of virtue. Many of his authorial comments are thus related to it. A considerable proportion of such remarks are about the ways of good officials and self-discipline. For instance, he highly praises Shang Yang, a high official of the State of Qin in the Period of Warring States, for his way of winning the trust of people, Feng Yi, who was known for his loyalty to the first emperor of the Eastern Han Dynasty, Meng Tian, a famous general in the Qin Dynasty, who committed suicide to show his loyalty to the emperor, Shen Jing, a general in the Eastern Jin Dynasty, who revenged his father's death, Shi Sunrui, a high official in the Eastern Han Dynasty, for his humbleness despite his outstanding service to the country, and Zhang Liang, a top advisor of the first emperor of the Western Han Dynasty, and Shen Tupan, an official and scholar in the Eastern Han Dynasty, for their wisdom in protecting themselves by declining high official positions or shying away from politics. All these are typical examples of faithfulness, loyalty, frugality, modesty, and self-discipline. On the other hand, he denounces Xie Fei and Xie Yue, officials in the Southern Dynasties, for their indifference to the murder of the emperor and inactivity as officials, Ji Shao, for serving the Jin Dynasty, which killed his father, and Feng Dao, a high official in the Five Dynasties, for serving ten emperors of five different dynasties without loyalty to any one of them. Through such examples he shows how to be a good son and a good official, how to conduct oneself in society. Those comments are the lessons that Sima Guang draws from historical facts and his advice for officials about the ways of conducting themselves in society. In this sense, *History as a Mirror for Governance* can also be regarded as a textbook of history for the feudal literati.

The literati of the Southern Song and the following dynasties have left behind many moving stories which fully demonstrated their esteem for *History as a Mirror for Governance*. For example, Hong Mai, a literary master of the Southern Song Dynasty, who was noted for his profound encyclopedic knowledge and research achievements in Confucian classics, history, philosophy, even medicine, divination, and astrology, admired Sima Guang and his book so much that he copied the book three times by hand. Later, he said in retrospect, "I was not able to recognize the merits and demerits of the book until I finished copying it for the third time." Another example was Zhao Ruyu of the Southern Song Dynasty, who was a member of the imperial family and served as Minister of Rites in charge of the Privy Council of Military Affairs in the reign of Emperor Guangzong. He taught his son to read the book when he was a small child and often said to him that "This book tells us what was behind the rise and fall of all the dynasties. Still another example was Zhu Xi's close friend Zhang Zhonglong, who, when staying in Chong'an County of Fujian Province, built a room on the left side of his bedroom in which there were nothing but several dozen cases of *History as a Mirror for Governance*. The room, named *"Mirror Study"*, was built for the sole purpose of reading this book. Later, Zhu Xi wrote an article specially to praise him for this when he learned about it.

In the Yuan and Ming Dynasties, when the status of Zhu Xi's *A General Outline of History as a Mirror for Governance* was over-raised and *History as a Mirror for Governance* itself was depreciated, there were much fewer scholars engaged in the study of it than in the Southern Song Dynasty. However, the book still enjoyed a number of faithful readers among the literati, especially in the early Yuan and late Ming Dynasties. In the early Yuan Dynasty, some of the scholars who had been subjects of the Southern Song Dynasty inherited the craze for the study of the book and used it as a means of expressing their patriotic feelings. Towards the end of the Ming Dynasty, due to the intensification of the social contradictions, the dynasty fell apart under the double blow of peasant uprisings and the invasion of the Qing army. Badly upset by the political situation, many scholars resorted to this book for ways of salvaging the nation, including, for example, Xue Yingqi and Wang Zongmu, two *jinshi* in the reign of Emperor Jiajing (1522–1566) who wrote sequels to the book.

In the Qing Dynasty, scholars like Gu Yanwu began to advocate the study of history for practical purposes. In the reign of Emperor Jiaqing (1769–1820), textual research became very popular. Many scholars broke through the tradition of favoring *A General Outline of History as a Mirror for Governance* over *History as a Mirror for Governance* since the Yuan and Ming Dynasties, and helped the latter regain its due status gradually.

According to *the Anecdotes of Hang Dazong* by Gong Zizhen, *History as a Mirror for Governance* was one of the four books that the renowned scholar Hang required his students to read when he was teaching at the Anding Academy of Classical Learning in Yangzhou, the other three being *General Institutions and Systems* by Du You, *A General Study of Historical Documents* by Ma Duanlin, and *A General History of China* by Zheng Qiao.

The keen scholarly interest in Sima Guang's book was also evidenced by the fact that many high-ranking officials wrote sequels to it, such as Xu Qianxue, who once served as the head of Ministry of Justice in the reign of Emperor Kangxi, and Bi Yuan, who was once governor-general of Hubei and Guangdong Provinces during the reign of Emperor Qianlong.

The admiration of the literati for *History as a Mirror for Governance* remained as deep as ever even in the late Qing Dynasty, when the political situation of the country was getting increasingly turbulent. A powerful provincial governor Zeng Guofan[1], for example, once expressed his

---

[1] Zeng Guofan (1811 – 1872), birth name Zeng Zicheng and courtesy name Bohan, a statesman, military general, and Confucian scholar of the late Qing Dynasty. He was also a voluminous writer.

commendation for the book, "Besides the six Confucian classics, one has but to master one of the seven books to be a scholar." The "seven books" here refer to *the Records of the Historian, the Book of the Han Dynasty, Zhuangzi, Essays of Han Yu, An Anthology of Poetry and Prose, the Origins of Chinese Characters*, and *History as a Mirror for Governance*.

In a letter to one of his followers Luo Shaocun, Zeng lavished his praises on *History as a Mirror for Governance*, "In my opinion, as far as the governance of the country is concerned, Sima Guang's book is unsurpassed by that of any other thinker of the past. One can widen his horizon by reading his insightful discussions on ancient history. His remarks about the division of the State of Jin by the States of Han, Zhao, and Wei towards the end of the Spring and Autumn Period, the usurpation of the Han Dynasty by the Wei Dynasty, the status of the Shu Han Dynasty as the legitimate successor of the Eastern Han Dynasty and so on, are all so convincing; its presentation of wars and battles and the gains and losses of both sides are so clear; his accounts of the vicissitudes of the families of some famous high-ranking officials and scholars are so inspiring and thought-provoking that no one could read it without being struck with awe because they are absent in any other book except the six classics. If you can learn the book by heart, you will have reliable guidelines to follow when you serve the country in any official position in the future." Zeng's esteem for the book is thus clearly expressed, and his comments on its merits are sufficient to show its profound influence on the literati.

Another scholar named Li Shuchang, one of the most well-known disciples of Zeng Guofan, who worked as a diplomat of the late Qing Dynasty to Britain, France, Germany, and Japan, wrote *A Proposed List of Eleven Books Published since the Zhou Dynasty for Officials*, which includes *History as a Mirror for Governance*. Some scholars even suggested that it be given the same status as that of the six Confucian classics.

Zhang Zhidong[1], another famous provincial governor of the Qing

---

[1] Zhang Zhidong (1837 – 1909), courtesy name Xiaoda and style name Xiangtao, a high-ranking official of the late Qing Dynasty. He was one of the leaders of the Westernization Movement.

Dynasty, also attached great importance to the book. In 1875, when he was the Education Commissioner of Sichuan Province, in order to encourage the students of the Sichuan Academy of Confucian Classics to work hard, he asked the renowned bibliographer Miao Quansun to give a reading list, who then came up with the four-volume *Questions and Answers about a Recommended List of Books*, which was to become an important reference book for students of history and literature. With over 2,000 ancient books on the list, the bibliography puts Sima Guang's book under the category of annals in a special sub-category called "*History as a Mirror for Governance* by Sima Guang and its Sequels". In the preface "Words of the Imperial Commissioner" which he wrote for Zhang, Miao said to the scholars of Sichuan, "In the study of history, one must follow the principle of advancing in proper order as well as that of perseverance. *History as a Mirror for Governance* and its sequels are by far the best for the learning of the general historical trend in the past dynasties." From this we can see Zhang's efforts in popularization of the book. Judging from his social status and influence, the lofty status of the book in the late Qing Dynasty must have gone beyond the boundaries of Sichuan Province. This was further evidenced by another anecdote: In the reign of Emperor Tongzhi (1862–1874), when the Jinling Publishing House sought scholarly opinion about the most publishable ancient books after it had decided to publish *Records of the Historian* and *the Book of the Han Dynasty*, a well-known bibliographer Mo Youzhi immediately gave his strong recommendation for Sima Guang's book.

It is thus not difficult to see that, thanks to the efforts of the Qing literati, the study of *History as a Mirror for Governance* regained popularity and the book became a must for scholars besides the six Confucian classics.

In 1923, a group of students of Tsinghua University who were going abroad to pursue academic studies, found themselves badly in need of acquiring some basic knowledge about studies of Chinese culture. So they asked Hu Shi and Liang Qichao to give them a list of recommended books. Hu wrote *A Minimum List of Books on Chinese History and Culture* in which he gave a fairly long list of history books on Chinese philosophy and literature, but none on Chinese history and culture. Liang Qichao criticized it as "wide of the mark" and wrote a book titled *A Basic Reader of Studies of Chinese Culture* with an appendix titled "A Minimum Bibliography" composed of four parts with nearly forty books, including *History as a Mirror for Governance* and the topically arranged histories of the Song, Yuan, Ming and Qing Dynasties. This bibliography, in his view, was a list of must-read books for studies of Chinese culture, as they best represented Chinese culture and were functionally the same as Zhang Zhidong's *Questions and Answers about a Recommended List of Books*.

The most important reason behind the high esteem of the literati for *History as a Mirror for Governance* was best stated by Hu Sanxing, "Without any knowledge of this book, an emperor would not know how to govern his people and prevent instability, an official would not know how to serve the emperor and help him govern the people, and the common people would not be able to do anything without bringing disgrace to their ancestors, still less to leave a name in history." Such profound influence of the book is undoubtedly convincing evidence of the great success of Sima Guang in achieving his aim.

3. Military Generals of the Feudal Dynasties and *History as a Mirror for Governance*

History as a Mirror for Governance also caught the keen interest of the military generals of the feudal dynasties. In the centuries that followed its publication, it was never short of admirers among the generals of the feudal governments and leaders of peasant uprisings. In their eyes, the book enjoyed equal status as such remarkable military works as *the Art of War by Sunzi, the Six Military Strategies* and *the Three Military Strategies*. These military generals had either learned the book by heart when they were young, or studied it whenever they were free during their military career. This was a unique phenomenon in Chinese history.

It is not difficult to understand all this, because the attraction of the book to the military generals lay mainly in its vivid descriptions of wars and battles.

The emphasis of *History as a Mirror for Governance* was on politics, and war is bloody politics or its continuation. It is, therefore, quite natural that the descriptions of wars constitute an important part of the book. Moreover, as this book was written in the annalistic style in imitation of *Zuo's Commentary*, Sima Guang himself said that "the narratives in this book should be like those in *Zuo's Commentary*". Since the latter was especially noted for its accounts of wars and was thus called "war annals", Sima Guang's book inherited this feature from it. Thus the accounts of wars had a special position in it.

The history of ancient China was one of incessant wars, including those between the ruling classes for power, those between armed forces of peasant uprisings and government armies, those between the Hans and other ethnic groups, as well as those between China and other countries. Such wars, which were directed by different commanders at different places and times, and in different forms and scales, produced different results. All those wars which took place in over one thousand years before the Song Dynasty were described in detail by Sima Guang, including the unification of China by Emperor Qinshihuang (221–210 B.C.), the expedition of Emperor Shizong of the Later Zhou Dynasty (951–960) to Huainan, the rebellion of the seven states (155 B.C.) in the Han Dynasty, the An Lushan-Shi Siming Rebellion (755–763) in the Tang Dynasty, the rebellion of Chen Sheng and Wu Guang (209 B.C.) in the Qin Dynasty, the rebellion of Huang Chao (848–884) in the Tang Dynasty, the punitive expedition of Emperor Wudi (140–87 B.C.) of the Han Dynasty on the Huns, the conquest of Tujue nationality by Emperor Taizong (627–649) of the Tang Dynasty, the conquest of the Qiang nationality, by Duan Ying in the Eastern Han Dynasty, and the invasion of Sichuan Province by Nanzhao regime in the Tang Dynasty. This might be attributable to Sima Guang's sympathy with the opinion of Du You (735–812), a politician and historian in the Tang Dynasty, that "the founding and destruction of a dynasty have always been the results of wars".

It is worth mentioning that the descriptions of the numerous wars in *History as a Mirror for Governance* were extremely vivid. Sima Guang was able to grasp the key factors of different wars and presented them differently, with detailed accounts of their causes and processes, as well as their consequences. There were both narratives of the general situations and descriptions of details, which greatly enhanced the readability of the stories of the historical figures.

In the recording of wars, one of the remarkable features of the book is the fact that it pays special attention to the military strategies and tactics of the generals. Gu Yanwu pointed out, "Along the lines of *Zuo's Commentary*, *History as a Mirror for Governance* records military strategies and tactics in great detail, including even those of the generals of the lost dynasties and rebels." Zeng Guofan also said once that the book "is noted for its clear analyses of the gains and losses of both sides of wars". Such examples can be found everywhere in the book. For instance, many events, such as the alliance of Sun Quan and Liu Bei in the Battle of Chibi against Cao Cao in the Period of Three Kingdoms (220–265), the doomed failure of Qi Jiong in the Disturbances of the Eight Princes (291–306) during the Western Jin Dynasty, the Southern Expedition of Fu Jian in the Former Qin Dynasty (350–394), and the moving of the capital by Emperor Xiaowendi of the Northern Wei Dynasty (386–557), are all recorded, including the meetings and plans beforehand, irrespective of whether they proved to be successful or not. Thus, the book is more profound and more instructive for later generations than most books.

With such unique features, military generals of later dynasties were naturally attracted to the book. Here we have to be contented with a few examples.

Among those military generals who suppressed the Taiping Uprising (1851–1864) there was a man named Hu Linyi[①], who became a *jinshi* after passing the highest imperial examination during the reign of Emperor Daoguang (1821–1950) and had suppressed a peasant uprising of the Miao

---

① Hu Linyi (1812 – 1861), courtesy name Kuangsheng and style name Runzhi, a scholar and official of the late Qing Dynasty.

ethnic group when he was prefect of Zhenyuan Prefecture of Guizhou Province. After the Taiping Uprising sparked off, he joined Zeng Guofan's army against the Taiping Army under imperial order and became one of Zeng's most capable generals as well as one of the best experts in history among Qing generals. Being a military strategist thoroughly familiar with *History as a Mirror for Governance*, he wrote a book *On Military Strategies in History*, which contained his reflections on history as well as his own military experiences. Besides, his outstanding performance in a number of battles against the Taiping Army might also have to do with what he had learned from Sima Guang's book.

Li Zicheng, the self-styled Daring King at the end of the Ming Dynasty, was a typical representative of those leaders of peasant uprisings who had benefited from *History as a Mirror for Governance*. According to *Brief Records of the Suppression of Rebellions* by Wu Weiye, a scholar at the turn of the Ming and Qing Dynasties, from the sixteenth year of the reign of Emperor Chongzhen (1643) when he established his rule in the city of Xiangyang, Li, "who was aware of his own ignorance, often ordered his officials to teach him reading and writing, and explain *History as a Mirror for Governance* to him, and often he made comments on it". Every day, he ordered his officials to teach him one chapter from one of the Confucian classics and a historical event. Born of a poor family, uneducated Li Zicheng took an interest in the book after he had made some major military victories, and even made some personal comments on it. Although the comments were not recorded, one can make a wise guess that they must have had to do with the lessons to be drawn from history, as well as military strategies and tactics.

Speaking of the love of military generals for *History as a Mirror for Governance*, it is necessary to mention those generals of the People's Republic of China. Of the founding fathers of the Republic, quite a few were familiar with history and military strategies and tactics. Marshal Chen Yi, for example, developed a keen interest in military books when he was young. His favorite books included *the Art of War by Sunzi*, *the Art of War by Wuzi*, *the Six Military Strategies*, and *the Three Military Strategies*, as well as *History as a Mirror for Governance*, which he considered must-read books for learning the ways of conducting oneself in society. Another example was Marshal Peng Dehuai. Although he had not had much schooling, he studied *the Romances of Three Kingdoms* and *the Water Margin* as well as Sima Guang's book when he was serving in the old army in his early years. When asked which books had influenced him most by the American journalist Edgar Snow in Yan'an, he replied that he had read *History as a Mirror for Governance* when he was young, which for the first time in his life urged him to think seriously about the social responsibilities of a soldier. Still another example was Marshal He Long, who persisted in his studies even after the founding of the Republic. In his bookcases one could find ancient books like *Records of the Historian*, *History as a Mirror for Governance*, and *A Brief Introduction to History as a Mirror for Governance*. From the words and deeds of these marshals one could easily perceive the profound influence of *History as a Mirror for Governance* on them.

4. Common People and *History as a Mirror for Governance*

When he was writing *History as a Mirror for Governance*, Sima Guang could not have included the common people in his putative readership. This, however, does not mean that no common people read the book later, nor does it mean that it would not exert any direct or indirect influence on the popular culture and mentality.

Needless to say, the common people's knowledge of the book was acquired mainly through the medium of popular historiography, which had been neglected by Chinese historians for a long time. For thousands of years, Chinese historians were all literati, and history books were accessible only to emperors, officials, and the literati. Things, however, began to change in the Southern Song Dynasty when the popularization of education gradually became the historical trend. A good proof was the appearance of children's primers such as *the Three-character Classic* by Wang Yinglin, which was accompanied by a similar trend in the field of history. Thus there appeared books like *History as a Mirror for Governance Topically Arranged* by Yuan Shu and *A General Outline of History as a Mirror for*

Governance by Zhu Xi, which were both adapted from Sima Guang's book. Obviously, these two books, especially the latter, were more suitable for learners of history than the original book. Thus the distance between the book and the common people was considerably narrowed. Wu Chenquan's *A Brief Introduction to History as a Mirror* in the Qing Dynasty was another milestone in the development of popular historiography.

Compared with *History as a Mirror for Governance*, any of the above three books undoubtedly enjoyed a much bigger readership, and exerted a much greater influence on the people, especially the common people. They cannot be equated to Sima Guang's book, but they were directly or indirectly adapted from it. Therefore, their influence on the thought and mentality of the common people was, to some extent, that of *History as a Mirror for Governance* itself, only they served as a medium between the book and the people.

Another way that made *History as a Mirror for Governance* more accessible to the common people in the feudal dynasties was the publication of abridged versions of the book. The first one of this kind was the sixty-volume *Abridged Version of History as a Mirror for Governance* written by Sima Guang himself, as he was afraid that the book might be too voluminous for ordinary readers. This book was soon followed by many different versions. A scholar named Zhang of the early Yuan Dynasty, for example, wrote in the postscript to an abridged version of the book published by Huimingxuan Press that scholars often read only some important parts of the book as they found it too time-consuming to cover the whole book. At the turn of the Song and Yuan Dynasties, there were already over a dozen commonly cited abridged versions, including the one-hundred-and-twenty-volume *An Annotated Abridged Version of History as a Mirror for Governance* by Lü Dazhu during the reign of Emperor Xiaozong (1163–1189) of the Song Dynasty, the one-hundred-volume *Excerpts from History as a Mirror for Governance* by an anonymous writer, the twenty-four-volume *Key Excerpts from History as a Mirror for Governance for Lü's Private School*, the thirty-volume *Shaowei's Comprehensive Excerpts from History as a Mirror for Governance* by Jiang Zhi, the thirty-volume *Essential Excerpts from History as a Mirror for Governance* by Cui

Dunshi, and the one-hundred-and-twenty-volume *Number One Scholar Lu's Abridged History as a Mirror for Governance with Annotations by One Hundred Scholars*, etc. These abridged versions of *History as a Mirror for Governance*, with only twenty to a little over one hundred volumes, were obviously much more succinct than the nearly three-hundred-volume original book.

In the Ming and Qing Dynasties, there appeared a number of new abridged versions of *History as a Mirror for Governance*. One of them was *the Essentials of History as a Mirror for Governance* published in the twenty-sixth year of the reign of Emperor Qianlong (1761), which consisted of a two-volume pre-sequel, a nineteen-volume body, and an eight-volume sequel. In other words, it had only nineteen volumes adapted from Sima Guang's book, just slightly over one-fifteenth of the latter. Such abridged versions were naturally more accessible to the common people.

It must be pointed out, however, that the most easily accessible and effective versions of *History as a Mirror for Governance* appeared in the 1950s. Soon after the founding of the People's Republic of China in 1949, Mao Zengdong and Zhou Enlai took a personal interest in the punctuating, collating, and publication of the book. In 1956, its first punctuated version was published, which removed a major barrier in its popularization. Meanwhile, abridged versions of the book like *Passages from History as a Mirror for Governance* selected and annotated by Qu Tuiyuan, *Selected Excerpts from History as a Mirror for Governance* annotated by Wang Zhongluo and others, and *One Hundred Stories from History as a Mirror for Governance* selected and annotated by Wang Mengqiao were reprinted many times. The first two, for example, had two editions with a total of over 143,500 copies, which was sufficient evidence of its influence, because most readers, unlike experts, learned about it through its abridged versions.

In recent years, a number of publishers have published various current vernacular versions of the book, which is doubtlessly another way of popularizing it as they are tailored to the needs of contemporary readers.

The popularity of *History as a Mirror for Governance* today can be further illustrated by statistics. In the nine centuries following its publication, the frequencies of its reprinting varied from period to period. It was printed only once in the last forty-four years of the Northern Song Dynasty, and reprinted once every five years in the Southern Song Dynasty, every nine years in the Yuan Dynasty, every twenty-three years in the Ming Dynasty, every twenty-nine years in the Qing Dynasty, every five years in the period from 1911 to 1949, while after the founding of the Republic of China in 1949 it has been reprinted once every three years. The numbers and frequencies of the reprints could be considered indications of the attention it has received in different periods.

It is worth mentioning that the unprecedented attention that the book has received since the 1950s is inseparable from the personal interest and endorsement of Mao Zedong. A great man of his time, Mao was at once a great revolutionary and an eminent scholar well versed in all kinds of ancient Chinese books ranging from classics and histories to novels and short stories. His greatest interest, however, lay in history books. He had read, for example, the forty-million-word *Twenty-four Histories*, *History as a Mirror for Governance*, *Sequel to History as a Mirror for Governance*, *A General Outline of History as a Mirror*, as well as the histories of all the feudal dynasties presented in separate accounts of important events. Besides, he had written numerous comments on these books. One of his favorite books was naturally *History as a Mirror for Governance*. In his private library, one can find not only the ancient thread-bound edition of the book, but also the punctuated paperback edition published by Shanghai Classics Publishing House in the 1950s, both of which are full of his hand-written comments.

Mao Zedong highly appraised *History as a Mirror for Governance*. In the winter of 1954, he said to the historian Wu Han when they were talking about the collation and punctuating of the book, "It is very well-written. Although it records history from the standpoint of the feudal ruling class, it presents a clear picture of the rise and fall of all the feudal dynasties. We can acquaint ourselves with historical events and draw lessons from them through critical reading." Thus we can see that Mao Zedong often urged the people to read this book because he hoped that they could learn about history and draw lessons from it. In short, he wanted "to use the past as a mirror for the governance of the country now."

Chapter Six

Conclusion

From the above discussions, we could reach the conclusion as follows. The annalistic style of historiography originated a long time ago in ancient China. It can be traced to *the Spring and Autumn Annals* by Kong zi, which established the principle of recording historical events in the order of date, month and year, which was an important milestone in the history of Chinese historiography. Later, it matured with the improvements by *Zuo's Commentary* and *the Chronicles of the Han Dynasty*.

The appearance of *the Records of the Historian* by Sima Qian brought about a profound change in ancient Chinese historiography, that is, the gradual replacement of the annalistic style by history presented in a series of chronicles and biographies as the mainstream of historiography. Consequently, the development of the annalistic style of historiography gradually slowed down and even halted after the Han Dynasty.

It was Sima Guang's *History as a Mirror for Governance* that revived this style of historiography and pushed it to a new height.

The book is acknowledged as a landmark in the development of ancient Chinese historiography after the publication of the *Spring and Autumn Annals, Zuo's Commentary* and *Records of the Historian*. It inherited and assimilated all the achievements and lessons in the writing of annals and, on the basis of this, further perfected this style of historiography creatively. Sima Guang's creative work involved not only its more rigorous style and narrative methodology, but also the verification of historical materials, and the writing of supplementary historical works. It can thus be said without exaggeration that *History as a Mirror for Governance* represented the highest achievement of the annals in ancient China. Just as Hu Yinglin of the Ming Dynasty put it, "The annalistic style of history reached its zenith with the publication of Sima Guang's book, which rendered all the works of its kind published before the Song Dynasty obsolete."

The indelible contributions of Sima Guang's *History as a Mirror for Governance* to Chinese historiography, nevertheless, lie more in its profound influence on the following generations than in the inheritance and development of his predecessors' achievements. Specifically, its influence is mainly reflected in the three aspects described below.

Firstly, the publication of the book promoted the rapid development of the annalistic style of historiography after the Song Dynasty. It gave new life to the annals whose development had come to a standstill due to the appearance of Sima Qian's *Records of the Historian*, which established the chronological-biographical style of historiography. The two different styles thus enjoyed equal status. Just as Wang Mingsheng[1] of the Qing Dynasty said, "The annalistic style before the Tang Dynasty was not even worth mentioning. It was not until the publication of *History as a Mirror for Governance* in the Song Dynasty that it gained equal status with the chronological-biographical style."

Secondly, the book not only perfected the annalistic style of historiography and set a pattern for later generations of annalists, but it also promoted the birth of new styles of historiography and boosted the flourishing of Chinese historiography after the Song Dynasty. The event-focus style of history established by Yuan Shu and the outline-focus style of history created by Zhu Xi not only promoted the flourishing of annals but also enriched the stylistic varieties of Chinese historiography. In the history of historiography, there are only three possible ways of recording history, i.e. the people-focused chronological-biographical history, the time-focused annals, and the event-focused history presented in separate accounts of important historical events. Yuan Shu's *History as a Mirror for Governance*

---

[1] Wang Mingsheng (1722 – 1798), courtesy name Fengjie and style name Xijiang, a historian and Confucian scholar of the Qing Dynasty. He applied his textual research approaches to the study of historiography.

Topically Arranged, being the first book of the third style, was an indelible contribution as it filled in a gap in Chinese historiography. Nevertheless, one cannot but admit that it was the product of the influence of *History as a Mirror for Governance*.

Thirdly, the publication of *History as a Mirror for Governance* brought with it a great number of related books and attracted Chinese scholars to engage in comprehensive studies of the book and other relevant history books, which gradually eventuated in a branch of learning called *History-Mirrorology*. After the Song Dynasty, sequels, abridged, imitating and adapted versions of the book emerged in a long succession, accompanied by numerous kinds of annotations, corrections, and criticisms. All these formed a comprehensive series with Sima Guang's book at the center. This unique phenomenon in the history of Chinese historiography was sufficient evidence of the profound and far-reaching influence of the book.

Furthermore, this book was also an intimate marriage of historiography and politics. Its influence on later generations, therefore, was not limited to the scope of historiography. In fact, it reached various aspects of society such as politics, culture, and people's mentality. From this book, people of all classes could learn Chinese history, draw lessons and get enlightenment from it about ways of conducting themselves in society. Lu Xun, a leading figure of modern Chinese literature, once remarked, "The theme of *A Dream of Red Mansions* varies from reader to reader. Scholars of Confucian classics see 'changes'; Confucian moralists see lust; gifted scholars see moving love stories; revolutionaries see repulsion for the Mandarin people; and gossipers see the secrets in the imperial palaces...." His whole point is that what one sees is determined by his social status and standpoint. The same is true of such a voluminous and profound magnum opus as *History as a Mirror for Governance*. From this book, people of different ages, social statuses and standpoints can get different inspirations. Nevertheless, there is still one common inspiration to them all, that is, the greatest value of history is the fact that it is a reservoirs of useful experiences and lessons of the past for future generations. In other words, "It tells stories of the past as a mirror for the future". The gains and losses in the governance of the country by the emperors in the past, and the ways in which the common people, officials, and literati conducted themselves, as well as the way scholars pursued their studies, can all serve as a mirror for people today to reflect on their own ways. In short, the lessons of ancient times can guide the social practice today. This history book, which is predominantly a political history of ancient China, has already exerted a tremendous influence on later generations, and will continue to do so in the future.

The influence of *History as a Mirror for Governance*, in fact, has already gone beyond the borders of China. With its various translated versions becoming available in other parts of the world, the studies of Sima Guang and the book by overseas scholars has also developed rapidly. The contemporary British Sinologist Edwin G. Pulleyblank, for instance, said that Sima Guang was truly a scientific historian, because he was the first one to attempt to establish truth on an objective basis. Meanwhile, he pointed out that, from the contemporary point of view, one of the most serious defects of his method, which almost all traditional Chinese historians committed, was his focus on isolated historical events and his failure to knit the individual events into a complicated web of relationships, as he only had some rather brief discussions of the causes and consequences of the events and the moral characters of the historical figures involved. In our view, it is not important whether this comment is correct or not. What matters is the fact that *History as a Mirror for Governance* has not only been treasured by the Chinese people, but it has received the increasing attention of international scholars as well, for any external attention is better than no attention at all. Indeed, one might wonder whether this history book has had any parallel in the history of world historiography.

Appendices

I. Bibliography

Bai Ting, *Quiet Talks from Zhanyuan* 白珽《湛渊静语》

Ban Gu, *Bibliography in the Book of the Han Dynasty* 班固《汉书·艺文志》; *Book of the Han Dynasty* 《汉书》

Bi Yuan, *Sequel to History as a Mirror for Governance* 毕沅《续资治通鉴》

Chen Bangzhan, *History of the Song Dynasty Topically Arranged* 陈邦瞻《宋史纪事本末》;

History of the Yuan Dynasty Topically Arranged 《元史纪事本末》

Chen He, *Chronicles of the Ming Dynasty* 陈鹤《明纪》

Chen Jingyun, *Corrections of Hu's Annotations of History as a Mirror* 陈景云《通鉴胡注举正》;

Errors in A General Outline of History as a Mirror for Governance 《纲目订误》

Chen Shou, *Records of the Three Kingdoms* 陈寿《三国志》

Chen Yuan, *A Tentative Study of Hu Sanxing's Annotations of History as a Mirror for Governance* 陈垣《通鉴胡注表微》

Chen Jing, *Sequel to History as a Mirror for Governance* 陈桱《通鉴续编》

Cui Dunshi, *Essential Excerpts from History as a Mirror for Governance* 崔敦诗《通鉴要览》

Cui Wanqiu, *A Study of History as a Mirror for Governance* 崔万秋《通鉴研究》

Du You, *General Institutions and Systems* 杜佑《通典》

Fan Xizeng, *Answers to Frequently Asked Questions about Important Books — a Revised Edition* 范希曾《书目答问补正》

Fan Ye, *Book of the Latter Han Dynasty* 范晔《后汉书》

Fei Shi, *Pronunciation of Words in History as a Mirror* 费氏《通鉴音释》

Feng Ban, *Corrections of A General Outline of History as a Mirror for Governance* 冯班《纲目纠谬》

Feng Zhishu, *Research on the Real Meanings of A General Outline of History as a Mirror for Governance* 冯智舒《纲目质实》

Gan Bao, *Annals of the Jin Dynasty* 干宝《晋纪》

Gao Shiqi, *Events in Zuo's Commentary Topically Arranged* 高士奇《左传纪事本末》

Gong Zizhen, *Anecdotes of Hang Dazong* 龚自珍《杭大宗逸事状》

Gu Xichou, *A Short Outline-Mirror of Official History* 顾锡畴《纲鉴正史约》

Gu Yingtai, *History of the Ming Dynasty Topically Arranged* 谷应泰《明史纪事本末》

He Zhong, *A Brief Analysis of History as a Mirror for Governance* 何中《通鉴纲目测海》；

　　　　A Tentative Study of A General Outline of History as a Mirror for Governance 《纲目测海》

Hong Mai, *Miscellaneous Notes from the Tolerant Study* 洪迈《容斋随笔》

Hu Cuizhong, *Sequel to the History of the Yuan Dynasty* 胡粹中《元史续编》

Hu Linyi, *On Military Strategies in History* 胡林翼《读史兵略》

Hu Sanxing, *An Analysis of the Mistakes in History as a Mirror for Governance* 胡三省《通鉴释文辨误》；

　　　　Expositions and Corrections of History as a Mirror for Governance 《资治通鉴释文辨误》；

　　　　Pronunciation and Annotations of History as a Mirror for Governance 《资治通鉴音注》

Hu Shi, *A Minimum List of Books on Chinese History and Culture* 胡适《一个最低限度的国学书目》

Hu Yigui, *Essentials of the Seventeen Histories* 胡一桂《十七史纂古今通要》

Hu Yin, *My Humble Opinions on Reading History* 胡寅《读史管见》

Hu Yuanchang, *A Research on the Books Cited by History as a Mirror for Governance* 胡元常《通鉴引用书目考》

Hua Zhanen, *Queries on A General Outline of History as a Mirror for Governance* 华湛恩《纲目志疑》

Huang Hongshou, *History of the Qing Dynasty Topically Arranged* 黄鸿寿《清史纪事本末》

Ji Yun, *An Annotated List of the Complete Library of Four Branches of Books* 纪昀《四库全书提要》

Jiang Liangji & Wang Xianqian, *Records of the East Flowery Country* 蒋良骐/王先谦《东华录》

Jiang Zhi, *Shaowei's Comprehensive Excerpts from History as a Mirror for Governance* 江贽《少微通鉴详节》

Jin Lüxiang, *Pre-sequel to A General Outline of History as a Mirror for Governance* 金履祥《纲目前编》;

　　　　Pre-sequel to History as a Mirror for Governance 《通鉴前编》

Li Tao, *Comprehensive Reflections on the Six Dynasties in History as a Mirror for Governance* 李焘《六朝通鉴博议》;

　　　　Draft of a Sequel to History as a Mirror for Governance 《续资治通鉴长编》

Li Tingji, *Dafang Outine-Mirror of History* 李廷机《大方纲鉴》

Li Xian, *Annotations of the Book of the Later Han Dynasty* 李贤《后汉书注》

Li Xinchuan, *Chronicles of Events Since the Jianyan Period* 李心传《建炎以来系年要录》

Li Youtang, *History of the Jin Dynasty Topically Arranged* 李有棠《金史纪事本末》;

　　　　History of the Liao Dynasty Topically Arranged 《辽史纪事本末》

Li Zhi, *Supplements to History from Jing Studio* 李冶《敬斋古今黈》

Liang Qichao, *Research Methodology in the Studies of Chinese History* 梁启超《中国历史研究法》

Liang Wudi, *General History* 梁武帝《通史》

Liu Ban, *Corrigenda of A History of the Eastern Han Dynasty* 刘攽《东汉刊误》;

　　　　Notes on History of the Han Dynasty by Three Lius 《三刘汉书标注》

Liu Shiju, *Chronicles of the Resurgence of the Song Dynasty-a Sequel to History as a Mirror for Governance* 刘时举《续中兴编年资治通鉴》

Liu Shu, *An Unofficial Sequel to History as a Mirror for Governance* 刘恕《通鉴外纪》

Liu Xisou, *Eternal Calendar* 刘羲叟《长历》

Liu Youyi, *Presentation of Events in A General Outline of History as a Mirror for Governance* 刘友益《纲目书法》

Liu Zhiji, *Generalities on History* 刘知幾《史通》

Ma Duanlin, *A General Study of Historical Documents* 马端临《通考》

Pei Songzhi, *Annotations on Records of the Three Kingdoms* 裴松之《三国志注》

Pei Yin, *Collected Expositions of the Records of the Historian* 裴骃《史记集解》

Qian Daxin, *Corrections of the Annotations of History as a Mirror* 钱大昕《通鉴注辨证》

Rui Changxu, *Supplementary Annotations of A General Outline of History as a Mirror for Governance* 芮长恤《纲目分注拾遗》

Shang Lu, *Sequel to A General Outline of History as a Mirror for Governance* 商辂《纲目续编》

Shen Chaoyang, *Remote History as a Mirror for Governance Topically Arranged* 沈朝阳《通鉴前编纪事本末》

Sheng Ruzi, *Talks on Study from Old Shu Studio* 盛如梓《庶斋老学丛谈》

Shi Zhao, *Annotations of History as a Mirror for Governance* 史炤《通鉴释文》

Sima Guang, *A Study of Different Versions of Historical Events in History as a Mirror for Governance* 司马光《通鉴考异》；

An Abridged Edition of History as a Mirror for Governance《通鉴节文》；

Biographies Emperors and Outstanding Officials in the Past Dynasties《历朝君臣事迹》；

Chronicles of Historical Events《历年图》；

Chronicles of the Bureaucratic Establishment《百官公卿表》；

Comprehensive Records《通志》；

Guide to the Use of History as a Mirror for Governance《通鉴释

例》；

History as a Mirror for Governance 《资治通鉴》；

Key Events in History as a Mirror for Governance 《通鉴举要历》；

Memorial for Submitting History as a Mirror for Governance 《进通鉴表》；

Notes on the History of the Song Dynasty by a Man from the Su River 《涑水记闻》；

Table of Contents of History as a Mirror for Governance 《通鉴目录》

Sima Kang, *Expositions of History as a Mirror* 司马康《释文》

Sima Qian, *Records of the Historian* 司马迁《史记》

Sima Zhen, *Collected Annotations of the Records of the Historian* 司马贞《史记索隐》

Wang Bai, *Guide to the Use of An Outline of History as a Mirror for Governance* 王柏《纲目凡例》

Wang Feng, *Subtle Meanings of A General Outline of History as a Mirror for Governance* 王峰《纲目发微》

Wang Fuzhi, *On History as a Mirror for Governance* 王夫之《读通鉴论》

Wang Guowei, *Collected Writings by Guantang* 王国维《观堂集林》

Wang Kekuan, *A Study of Different Versions of the Guides in A General Outline of History as a Mirror for Governance* 汪克宽《通鉴纲目凡例考异》

Wang Shizhen, *The Outline-Mirror of Historical Events* 王世贞《纲鉴会纂》

Wang Yinglin, *A Comprehensive Interpretation of Geography in History as a Mirror for Governance* 王应麟《通鉴地理通释》；

Records of Observances from Arduous Studies 《困学纪闻》

Wang Youxue, *Collected Readings of A General Outline of History as a Mirror for Governance* 王幼学《纲目集览》

Wu Chengquan, *A Simplified Outline-Mirror of History* 吴乘权《纲鉴易知录》

Wu Weiye, *Brief Records of the Suppression of Rebellions* 吴伟业《绥寇纪略》

Xi Zaochi, *Annals of the Han and Jin Dynasties* 习凿齿《汉晋春秋》

Xia Xie, *History of the Ming Dynasty as a Mirror for Governance* 夏燮《明通鉴》

Xu Qianxue, *Reedit of Sequels to History as a Mirror for Governance* 徐乾学《资治通鉴后编》

Xu Zhaowen, *A Textual Research on A General Outline of History as a Mirror for Governance* 徐昭文《纲目考证》

Xue Yingqi & Wang Zongmu, *History of the Song and Yuan Dynasties: a Sequel to History as a Mirror for Governance* 薛应旗/王宗沐《宋元资治通鉴》

Xun Yue, *Annals of the Han Dynasty* 荀悦《汉纪》

Yan Shigu, *Annotations of the Book of the Han Dynasty* 颜师古《汉书注》

Yan Yan & Tan Yunhou, *Supplements to History as a Mirror for Governance* 严衍-谈允厚《资治通鉴补》

Yang Longrong, *History of the Three Feudatories Topically Arranged* 杨隆荣《三藩纪事本末》

Yang Zhongliang, *History of the Imperial Song Dynasty As a Mirror for Governance Topically Arranged* 杨仲良《皇宋通鉴长编纪事本末》

Ye Xianggao, *Yutang Outline-Mirror of History* 叶向高《玉堂纲鉴》

Yin Qixin, *Exposition of a General Outline of History as a Mirror for Governance* 尹起莘《纲目发明》

Yu Shenxing, *A Gist of the Outline-Mirror of History* 于慎行《纲鉴要编》

Yuan Hong, *Annals of the Latter Han Dynasty* 袁宏《后汉纪》

Yuan Hui, *Records of History by Topics* 元晖《科录》

Yuan Liaofan, *Yuan Liaofan's Supplement to the Outline-Mirror of History* 袁了凡《袁了凡纲鉴补》

Yuan Shu, *History as a Mirror for Governance Topically Arranged* 袁枢《通鉴纪事本末》

Zhang Chong, *Events in Spring and Autumn Annals and Zuo's Commentary Topically Arranged* 章冲《春秋左氏传事类本末》

Zhang Geng, *Underlying Meanings and Corrections of A General Outline of History as a Mirror for Governance* 张庚《纲目释地纠谬》; *Underlying Meanings and Supplementary Notes on A General Outline of History as a Mirror for Governance* 《纲目释地补注》

Zhang Jian, *History of the Western Xia Dynasty Topically Arranged* 张鉴《西夏纪事本末》

Zhang Pu, *Comments on the Past Dynasties* 张溥《历代史论》;

Preface to the Reprint of History as a Mirror for Governance Topically Arranged 《重刊通鉴纪事本末序》

Zhang Shi, *Sincere Comments from History as a Mirror for Governance* 张栻 《通鉴论笃》

Zhang Shoujie, *Correct Meanings of the Records of the Historian* 张守节《史记正义》

Zhang Xu, *History-Mirrorology* 张须《通鉴学》

Zhang Xuhou, *A Study of History as a Mirror for Governance* 张煦侯《通鉴学》

Zhao Shaozu, *Discussion about the Annotations of History as a Mirror* 赵绍祖 《通鉴注商》

Zhao Shiji, *The Outline-Mirror of the Dynasties* 赵时济《纲鉴统宗》

Zheng Qiao, *A General History of China* 郑樵《通志》

Zhu Lin, *A Brief Outline-Mirror of History* 朱璘《纲鉴辑略》

Zhu Xi, *A General Outline of History as a Mirror for Governance* 朱熹《资治通鉴纲目》

Zou Shurong, *Random Notes on A General Outline of History as a Mirror for Governance* 邹树荣《纲目随笔》

Zuo Qiuming, *Zuo's Commentary* 左丘明《左传》

A Basic Reader of Studies of Chinese Culture 《国学入门书要目及其读法》

A Bibliography of Canons and Literature of the New Book of the Tang Dynasty 《新唐书·艺文志》

A Sequel to A General Outline of History as a Mirror for Governance 《纲目续麟》

A Synoptic Catalogue of the Complete Library of Four Treasuries 《四库全书总目》

An Annotated Abridged Version of History as a Mirror for Governance 《吕大著点校增节备注资治通鉴》

Authorized Version of A General Outline of History as a Mirror for Governance 《御批通鉴纲目》

Authorized Version of Selected Readings from A General Outline of History as a Mirror for Governance 《御批通鉴辑览》

Bibliographies of Classics and Books in the Book of the Sui Dynasty 《隋书·经籍志》

Essentials of History as a Mirror for Governance 《通鉴揽要》

Gongyang's Commentary 《公羊传》

Guliang's Commentary 《谷梁传》

Key Excerpts from History as a Mirror for Governance for Lü's Private School 《吕氏家塾通鉴节要》

Number One Scholar Lu's Abridged History as a Mirror for Governance with Annotations by One Hundred Scholars 《陆状元集百家注资治通鉴详节》

Spring and Autumn Annals 《春秋》

The Art of War by Sunzi 《孙子兵法》

The Bamboo Annals 《竹书纪年》

The Six Military Strategies 《六韬》

The Third Edition of A General Outline History as a Mirror for Governance 《通鉴纲目三编》

The Three Military Strategies 《三略》

True Records of the Qing Dynasty 《清实录》

II. Glossary

Academy of Scholarly Worthies 集贤院 (jí xián yuàn) 44

anecdotes 故事 (gù shì) 43, 56, 62, 121

annalistic style 编年体 (biān nián tǐ) 2, 8, 9, 10, 11, 12, 13, 14, 15, 17, 19, 20, 21, 24, 25, 26, 27, 29, 36, 38, 46, 47, 54, 56, 57, 81, 83, 84, 85, 86, 89, 90, 93, 94, 103, 125, 132, 133

annals 编年史 (biān nián shǐ) 2, 7, 8, 9, 10, 11, 12, 13, 14, 15, 16, 17, 19, 20, 21, 22, 23, 24, 25, 26, 27, 28, 29, 36, 43, 46, 47, 48, 49, 50, 52, 54,

philosophical books 诸子 (zhū zǐ) 1

records of emperors' activities 起居注 (qǐ jū zhù) 1

records of officials of the past dynasties 职官 (zhí guān) 1

records 书 (shū) 1

Spring and Autumn style 春秋笔法 (chūn qiū bǐ fǎ) 1

table of contents 丛目 (cóng mù) 1

tables 表 (biǎo) 1

tablet inscriptions 碑碣 (bēi jié) 1

textual research 考据学 (kǎo jù xué) 1

The superiorman remarks 君子曰 (jūn zǐ yuē) 1

three institutes of Heavenly Manifestations 天章三馆 (tiān zhāng sān guǎn) 1

unofficial histories 杂史 (zá shǐ) 1

unofficial history books 别史 (bié shǐ) 1